FOR ALL
Eternity

A Story of Heaven

J.C. GOTTLIEB

Copyright © 2023 J.C. Gottlieb.

All rights reserved. No part of this book may be reproduced, stored, or transmitted by any means—whether auditory, graphic, mechanical, or electronic—without written permission of both publisher and author, except in the case of brief excerpts used in critical articles and reviews. Unauthorized reproduction of any part of this work is illegal and is punishable by law.

ISBN: 979-8-88640-725-9 (sc)
ISBN: 979-8-88640-726-6 (hc)
ISBN: 979-8-88640-727-3 (e)

Because of the dynamic nature of the Internet, any web addresses or links contained in this book may have changed since publication and may no longer be valid. The views expressed in this work are solely those of the author and do not necessarily reflect the views of the publisher, and the publisher hereby disclaims any responsibility for them.

One Galleria Blvd., Suite 1900, Metairie, LA 70001
1-888-421-2397

But the souls of the just are in the hand of God, and no torment shall touch them.

They seemed, in the view of the foolish, to be dead; and their passing away was thought an affliction and their going forth from us, utter destruction.

But they are in peace.

For if before men, indeed, they be punished, yet is their hope full of immortality;

Chastised a little, they shall be greatly blessed, because God tried them and found them worthy of himself.

—Wisdom 3:1–5

For Claire, Olivia, and
Bill, with love.

CONTENTS

Acknowledgments ix
Introduction xi

Chapter 1	The End	1
Chapter 2	The Beginning	10
Chapter 3	Introductions	18
Chapter 4	Babies in Heaven	30
Chapter 5	Battle of the Bands in the Sky	38
Chapter 6	Bears, Bears, Bears	48
Chapter 7	Memories	59
Chapter 8	Volcanoes and Values	67
Chapter 9	Catherine of Siena	76
Chapter 10	Period Differences	87
Chapter 11	Old Bethlehem	94
Chapter 12	A Family Christmas	108
Chapter 13	Winter Trekking	115
Chapter 14	Back on Earth	121
Chapter 15	Melody	136
Chapter 16	A Romance Novel	144
Chapter 17	A Coping Strategy	155
Chapter 18	Melody's Problem	164
Chapter 19	Healing Weekend	173

Epilogue 185

ACKNOWLEDGMENTS

Special thanks to Aggie and Bob, who encouraged me from the beginning, and to Fred, who has stood by me and taken care of our family for forty-two years.

Many thanks also to the staff of A Woman's Answer Medical Center in Gainesville, Florida.

INTRODUCTION

On June 4, 1999, the worst thing that a mother could imagine happened to me: one of my children was hit by a car and killed. Our oldest daughter was now gone out of our lives forever. At all the family gatherings—Thanksgiving, Christmas, birthdays— there would be a big gaping hole in our family circle. Before it happened, I had just begun cultivating a very close relationship with God, and I had been working on learning his will for me so that I could gear my life in his direction. In the wee hours of June 5, however, my heart physically closed up tight, not wishing to explode into a thousand pieces after facing this huge loss. Unfortunately, it would not open again after that to let in the warmth and comfort of God's love.

The story that follows comes from God. Longing for his comfort, I started praying like before. After several months, he revealed to me the visions of the world depicted in this story. I believe he was helping me accept the awful reality that I had to accept before I could go on. Now, after a year of putting these wonderful thoughts down on paper, I sense my heart muscle softening to accept his holy presence and love again. Of course, it means I must face a reality that is difficult to face, but because of his loving guidance, I can face it, knowing that my daughter is safe with him.

This book represents two faith journeys. The first is my real-life journey led by my God; the second is the fictional one where my daughter learns to accept her place in creation. I have no way of knowing what she really is doing in heaven, but I believe the thoughts and dreams depicted in the following narrative are one way of representing a heaven that is understandable to our human minds. I also believe the Holy Spirit has revealed these ideas to me as a source of comfort for others as well.

—J. C. Gottlieb
Spring 2000

After writing about 120 pages of my daughter's activities in heaven and on earth, I found that I was unable to put an ending to the story. For years, I wondered how it would end. Any ideas I had didn't really work. I knew that the story would be finished in God's time, so I wasn't worried. Finally, this past summer, the Holy Spirit came to my assistance again and suggested the ending that I've written. I believe I have his support in this, and I hope that I've done it justice.

—J. C. Gottlieb
December 2015

CHAPTER 1

The End

I woke up early on June 4, 1999. I was feeling optimistic about the future and was anxious to start working on my new career plan. I had filled my calendar with all kinds of activities to help me prepare for my future profession. Until then, I had seen myself doing something with the environment for the rest of my life. Since I love the natural world—and it's pretty messed up—I had wanted to help people appreciate every aspect of it, so they would want to take care of our planet.

My new plan would take me out of nature and into hospital wards. I was going to study music therapy. I would be cheering up very sick patients with music. I could still enjoy nature in my free time. In fact, I planned to raise my children to appreciate it, too. Maybe I'd become a Scout leader. But music therapy was going to be my profession.

As I showered that morning, I thought of all the experiences that had taken me through a nightmarish five-year struggle toward this new and exciting career path. There had been days and weeks at a time in hospital psych wards, extensive counseling sessions, group sessions, endless trials with antidepressants, and lots of confusion. I had just completed a six-week course intended to help me stop cutting and burning myself. I didn't understand why I should stop since it was my own body, but I tried anyway, to please my family. Dressing in front of my full-length mirror, I looked at my scarred-up body in a new light.

"Finally, this is finished," I told myself. "I have a plan. I know who I am and what I want, and I feel good for the first time in years. These are my battle scars."

While combing out the tangles in my long hair, I remembered how Kathy told me it was the color of dog poop. She thought she was funny, but I took it to heart and dyed it all kinds of colors.

"None of that, Iris," I said out loud. "Even dirty blonde won't do. From now on, your hair is golden brown." I smiled at that. Nothing about me was bad.

The years from nineteen to twenty-four are supposed to be fun. Halcyon years. Not for me. They were years of hard lessons and crippling depression. I wanted to die and leave this world behind. But now, I had every reason to go on living.

I dressed casually, choosing my favorite T-shirt, an orange one with a bright yellow tie-dyed sun on the front. I pulled on my cutoffs and stepped into my purple Converse sneakers. As I slid my glasses onto my nose, I watched my true blue eyes uncross. I flung my hair back behind my shoulders and stood up straight. I was ready to face the day.

As I went into the kitchen to get breakfast, Sara came running out from under the bed. I would've liked it if she had slept with me *in* bed, but for some reason, she chose to sleep under it. Sara was a rescue cat a friend had given me. She was old and had thyroid cancer, so she was skinny and always hungry. I really didn't need a cat, especially not one who needed veterinary care, but I've always been a softie for animals, so I didn't have the heart to give her away. She croaked out her meow and chased me around the kitchen, demanding her breakfast.

I used to struggle to give her a pill twice a day. I would squeeze the back of her jaw and slip a finger in the side to keep her mouth open, and then I'd push the pill in. No matter how long I held her mouth shut, she always managed to spit the pill out when I let go. She fought me tooth and nail—literally! When I explained my problem to my grandmother, she suggested that I just hide the pill in Sara's food.

"She gobbles that up fast enough," Mémère added.

Why didn't I think of that? After that, I didn't have any trouble at all. I just put the pill in her food, and she licked the plate clean.

After feeding Sara, I was free to get my own breakfast of peanut butter toast with strawberry jam. I washed it down with a glass of milk, took my pills, and grabbed my guitar to practice. I was learning a lot about jazz in my class at the community college, and I practiced as much as possible, especially since I had decided to make music my life. Sara cleaned up my breakfast crumbs on the couch, washed herself, curled up beside me, and purred peacefully.

While practicing, I went over my plans for the day. I was putting off calling Mémère for a ride. She never complained, but I figured, she'd like some peace and quiet sometimes. I wished I didn't have to call on her so much, but Mom and Papa were in Georgia.

The first thing on my agenda was a meeting downtown with a guy named Mike. He wanted to help me with the VA Hospital's Fourth of July celebration, and I had agreed to meet him at noon at the Keg and Trough. I had learned to organize events when I was a Senior Girl Scout, so I volunteered to plan the entertainment for the veterans. That would tie in nicely with my music therapy plans.

After that, I had to be at the local hospital at one-thirty to meet with the band that was playing on the bone marrow unit that day. I couldn't pedal all the way from downtown to the hospital in just half an hour, so I needed Mémère to drive me. After the hospital, I had my appointment with Sandra, my very cool therapist. That was a couple of miles away from the hospital, but I had until four, so I figured I could bike there in time. No need to ask for a ride.

Mike didn't show up at the Keg and Trough. I sat down on the curb outside the pub and waited for Mémère. I practiced my guitar while waiting. Lots of people walked by, and I was proud of the fact that I could talk calmly to anyone who approached me. (Well, let's say, I hid my self-consciousness and pretended to be calm. Anyway, it worked.)

Even before I got the bike in her car, Mémère started in on me.

"Iris, you're doing too much," she said. "Take it easy, or you'll get sick again."

Just a couple of months before, she was telling me to get out of the house and do things. Now I was doing too much. Jeesh! Would I ever please her? But I knew she meant well and didn't say what I was thinking. At the hospital, I ran into her pastor in the elevator. He didn't know me—I never went to church or anything—but I told him who my grandmother was, and he knew her right away. I told him about my plans, and he wished me blessings. That was dorky, but I thanked him anyway.

I got off on the bone marrow floor, and the band members were waiting for me. They introduced themselves, and we all went into the isolation unit to do my very first gig. The patients loved us. After a few songs, Brenda, the bandleader, introduced me as their newest member. She asked me what my favorite church hymn was. That threw me off. I wondered what to say. Then I remembered Ani DiFranco, my favorite singer, sings "Amazing Grace," which is indeed a hymn, and I love that one, so I said that was my favorite. We sang that, and our audience loved it too.

I really enjoyed myself with the band, and the surprising thing was that they enjoyed having me there. (When I was depressed, I never considered the possibility of anyone enjoying having me around.) It made me feel even better about my decision to make this my life's work. And, to tell the truth, I was comfortable with the whole thing. Downright happy, in fact.

As we left the bone marrow unit, Brenda invited me to come downtown to see them play at the battle of the bands that evening. They were scheduled to play at eight o'clock, and I said I thought I could make it. The only problem was going to be getting home after dark. My parents didn't want me riding my bike after dark, and although I made a big deal about them being too bossy, deep down, I agreed with them. I'd have to call Mémère again.

But first, I pedaled to Sandra's office. We had found her when my mom first took me to Gainesville. My folks were living in Germany at the time, compliments of the US Army.

(They had actually checked out a residential program over there for me, but I wasn't comfortable with that. My German wasn't what it used to be when I was a little kid, and I knew I'd have to express feelings that I didn't have the words for.) Gainesville had a pretty good support system for mental health patients, and besides, my grandparents were living there, as well as a few aunts and uncles.

When I got to Sandra's office, it was already thundering. We were going to have one of those torrential downpours that happen around four o'clock on summer days in Gainesville. Sandra was happy to hear how well I was doing and encouraged me to keep my schedule busy. The rain started pounding on the roof, and we both had to yell part of the time. I didn't get frustrated. In fact, Sandra and I both burst out laughing together once. Laughing didn't happen often in those days, but when it did, it felt really good. After my hour, Sandra's receptionist gave me a trash bag and helped me wrap it around my guitar/backpack. I rode home with mud splashing from my rear tire onto the covered backpack and into my hair. It wasn't cold—steam was actually rising from the hot pavement—but it was disgusting.

I had to majorly clean up when I got home. The hot shower felt good, and it was nice to put on fresh clothes. Sara looked at me hopefully when I came out of the bathroom, and I zipped into the kitchen to get her some supper. I had some leftover beans and rice in the fridge, which I ate cold while calling Mémère.

"I'll have to get you at nine. Is that okay?" I hesitated, thinking that was awfully early.

"You can bring your PJs and toothbrush and stay overnight. We'd be happy to have you," Mémère added.

An overnight would be nice. Grandpa always made delicious pan fries with bacon and eggs for breakfast, and they always gave me a big glass of orange juice to drink.

"That would be nice," I said, smiling. I decided I would come home right after breakfast and sit with Sara in the morning.

Then I called Brenda. She wasn't home of course, but I left a message saying I was running late and wouldn't make it to their act, but I hoped to see them afterward.

I grabbed my giant pill case off the table. Right next to it was my Swiss Army knife. I felt a pang of guilt as I remembered how I had slipped up and cut myself the other day after sharpening the blade. I sighed and put the pillbox in my backpack with my pajamas and toothbrush. Each day was a struggle. I would have to remember not to sharpen and oil the knife so often. Maybe I could plan to do it just before I had to leave the house…

As I fastened the lights on my bike, Sara ran to the door to see what was up.

"I'll sit with you tomorrow. I promise," I said as I slipped out. I managed to get the door shut just before she escaped.

It was already eight o'clock. I had to get downtown as quickly and as safely as possible. Gainesville is tricky for bikers and pedestrians. There are large intersections with four or five lanes of traffic in each direction. There are also quieter spots, where you can work your way across more easily. You really have to watch out. When you're on a bike, lots of drivers don't even see you. I chose an intersection where I would have to cross about six lanes, but the street I was crossing from didn't continue on the other side. It ended in a *T*, which meant I'd have less traffic to watch out for.

My little cross street had a red light, and I should have waited for green, but the eastbound lanes were empty, so I rode in the crosswalk to the center strip. There were only a few cars going west, but the setting sun was shining in the eyes of the drivers coming toward me. After the last car passed, I rode out into the road. The sun had kept me from noticing another car behind the one with its lights on. (I had learned about that in a driving class in Germany.) It's all so easy to understand now. I was anxious to get to the battle of the bands and wasn't as cautious as I should have been. I saw the car right after I rode out into the street and pedaled hard to get out of its way, but it was too late.

The car hit my rear tire hard enough that the bike and I went flying into the air. By the time I hit the road, people were rushing to help me. I couldn't breathe. Someone cut the chin strap of my helmet, and that helped. I started to hurt all over. That did it for me. I lashed out at God. I mean, I wasn't a believer, but I knew enough about him to blame him.

I can't believe this! I have had the rottenest luck all my life! I can't die now. My life is finally starting to mean something, and I have to get hit by a car? God, why did you have to let this happen?

Then I saw the tunnel.

Oh, no! It's that stupid tunnel with the light at the end of it. Get these old relatives out of here! I refuse to go! I'm going back to where I belong.

I returned to my body. I don't know how I did that, but I was back in the road and being lifted onto a stretcher.

But I wasn't finished with God.

God, I don't get it. When I laid down in the slush in the middle of the street in Ashland, you didn't let a car come and run over me. You didn't even let me get pneumonia and die. I had to go back and fight the depression. And now? Now that I've got the depression almost licked, now you let me get run over. What is it with you? Does everything have to be your way? Can't my plans count for anything? I don't even believe in you!

How am I supposed to deal with this? Will I ever be okay again? Is this going to ruin my plans? You know how important using music to cheer people up is to me. And do you remember how I held out against suicide because I didn't want to hurt my family? Now what? Now they have to deal with my death anyway? What is your goal here? None of this makes sense!

Mémère! I wonder what time it is. I have to get a message to her. Ugh! I can't talk! There's something in my mouth…

And that's when I died and came to heaven. No more chance to return to earth.

CHAPTER 2

The Beginning

I was in a dream world. There was a swirling fog, like the fog we used to make in the witch's cauldron at Halloween. Only this was more. You would need a lot of dry ice to make this much. I saw the tunnel with a hazy light at the end. And all our dead relatives were lined up on both sides, eagerly signaling for me to go in the direction of the light. I remember wondering if I was really dead. It looked pretty conclusive. I didn't want to be dead. I had just gone through all that uncontrollable depression and had finally found some joy in my life. It was the worst kind of irony.

Sandra always said that I should express my feelings. I started to kick and scream and swing at the fog. I was really desperate. I heard thunder and saw a flash of lightning. Had I caused that? I let off a couple more screaming fits, which were followed by thunder and lightning. That made me feel better, but now I had drifted much closer to the light. I started rising weightlessly in midair. I was scared that I was indeed dead, and I considered it grossly unfair.

"Life isn't fair!" It was my mom's reflex answer whenever one of us said something wasn't fair. I automatically heard her voice in my head, and I could picture her defensive expression as she said it.

"Mommy, I'm scared. I need you with me now." It seemed like nothing had ever gone my way, and I started crying, feeling so sorry for myself.

Then I found myself waiting in line.

In line for what? Don't tell me this is gonna be the big judgment. Well, I don't care. I tried and tried and tried. This is what you get, God. I did my best. If you exist, then you made me—and you can deal with all my problems now. I just don't care.

I wondered about all the other people waiting with me. It was a large space. Not a room. It's hard to describe. All whiteness. There were people from all over the world around me. All dead, I supposed. There were plenty of Africans, which was no surprise, with all the droughts over there.

Why does a loving, caring, all-powerful God let bad things happen to innocent people? Even babies? The only thing they did wrong was to be born in the wrong place.

There were also Muslims there. I could tell the women by their veils. Hijabs. And standing right next to them were Jewish men, dressed all in black, complete with banana curls hanging down in front of their ears, and those hard black hats on their heads. Everyone seemed a little dazed. Like me. They were probably wondering what was going to happen next. I wondered what the real God would look like. Who would win out? There had been wars over this question. Not that people didn't know; they just fought each other because they believed theirs was the real one and the others were worshiping the wrong one.

Will the real God please stand up?

For me, it turned out to be Jesus. He looked just like I had pictured him in Catholic school. Only the real person was better. I thought he was glowing, but maybe not. There was just something about him that took my breath away. It may have been his eyes. I felt them piercing right into my inner being. Like he was finding my deepest, darkest secrets, reading my soul. I thought I should feel vulnerable, but I didn't. It was like I couldn't do anything wrong in his eyes. He just plain loved me.

"Such a rage, Iris. You were not anxious to join us, I take it." His voice was gentle and understanding.

Duh…and then I answered, "I had plans for my life. I had lost five years, and I was ready to get going. There was so much unfinished business."

"Yes, there always is." He had a faraway look in his eyes. For a split second, he looked sad. He looked at me and said, "There's not much we can do when you ride out in front of moving traffic. You did have a red light, you know." He wasn't mad or anything. His voice was gentle, like he was going to take me in his arms and hold me.

"Did the storm over your sister's island help to release some of your frustration? Claire sensed that it was you."

I was kind of happy to hear that the thunder-storm had been over Saint Thomas. If I could only say goodbye to one person on earth, I'd want it to be Claire. I wondered how she had found out, and I wondered if anyone else knew.

"I promise you, you will come to like it here, and all your sorrow at leaving the world will be a thing of the past. You were not supposed to return to us this early. We had big plans for you, too. But there's a lot of evil in the world. There have been obstacles placed in front of you ever since your birth."

I had been blaming God for all the bad things that had happened in my life, and here he was telling me that he really wanted me to live and do good things with my life. It was hard to swallow.

"This time, you were really on the right path, Iris," Jesus continued. "Your new career choice would have led to the salvation of many souls. Music therapy is one of the reasons why we gave humans the ability to appreciate the beauties of sound, sight, and touch. If they were in deep despair or even just a little sad, the beauties experienced by the senses would give them renewed hope. And you would have been one of the ones to instill this hope. That would have given you great joy and peace because you have a kind heart."

"So you didn't plan my death?" I asked, not wanting to believe it.

"No, Iris. Death happens. We know what will happen, but most of the time, we choose not to interfere with nature. People must know that when they go out in front of a car, there will be natural consequences."

I thought about that. If God is all-powerful and he knows what's going to happen, why can't he just adjust things a little? Doesn't he have control over everything that goes on?

He must've read my thoughts because he said, "We do adjust things, but as much as possible, we do it in the natural order. For instance, we could have had you leave your apartment a few seconds later. Maybe Sara would have run out and you would have had to catch her. Or maybe one of your neighbors would have stopped and talked to you. We do these things all the time to prevent accidents, but this time, we decided that you had had enough problems in your short life, and we chose to give you the shortcut."

I need to add here that nothing Jesus had said up to that point had placated me. I was still very angry about having died. And when he said that about the shortcut, I pictured the three of them—Father, Son, and Holy Spirit—sitting around a conference table, discussing what to do with me.

"We'll just give her the shortcut."

What gave them the right to decide such a thing? It was *my* life, and they were making a decision to end it, willy-nilly. And then acting like they were doing me a favor! What were they thinking? It made me even madder. It took me a long time to cool down to the point where I could talk.

"How about my family? My friends?" My voice betrayed my feelings. I took a deep breath. "How are they going to cope with this?"

"They will not be the first to lose a loved one, as you say," Jesus answered. "They'll survive this, and they'll be stronger for it. You mustn't worry about things on earth anymore. When you've discarded all traces of human weakness, there will be work for you here in heaven. Someday, your family will join you here, and you'll be able to help them make the transition to the spiritual world, if you choose. In fact, a relative of yours has requested to be your guide until you are adjusted to heaven. He will join you shortly."

I had just arrived in a new world, and I wanted to understand, but I couldn't. Jesus was telling me heaven was different, and this relative of mine was going to help me get used to being a spirit. Fine. But as he spoke, I had a burning question that I just had to ask.

"But, Jesus," I just blurted it out. "Why are you being nice to me? I don't even believe in you."

"Don't worry about that, Iris." He actually smiled. "We are the judge of all men, and we know what is in your heart even better than you do. You were created to do good while on earth, but your life was shortened. Now we need for you to do our work here in heaven."

Suddenly, I felt a glowing warmth all over. I looked, and my body was healed! All my battle scars were gone, and my hair was really long and soft and its natural golden-brown color. The best part was that my mind was completely clear. No more drugged-up feeling.

"You still don't believe?" Jesus said with a touch of gentle sarcasm. "Your Uncle Mike was given a vision of you right at the moment of your restoration."

Uncle Mike. Would he tell my parents that I was okay? Probably.

A little while later, after I had calmed down a little, I was sitting alone on a stump in a garden that I had made, just wishing for things to appear here and there. It was therapeutic to be there, quiet and alone. Because I had planned it myself and had made my own improvements as I went along, it turned out to be the most beautiful garden I had ever seen. There were fresh spring flowers everywhere, and butterflies were fluttering all around the flowers. I looked for a hummingbird and found one right away. (*Kolibri* was the German word that came to me. Papa was the first to show me one, and he taught me the word.) I closed my eyes and listened. It was so peaceful, and it really made me feel good, deep down inside. There was a mockingbird singing. I wished I could whistle like Papa and see if the mockingbird would try to repeat my song.

With God, all things are possible, and here I am in heaven…

I puckered up and tried the complicated whistle. It turned out very similar to Papa's. The mockingbird turned its head toward me and made an attempt to repeat it. I whistled again. This time, the mockingbird's reply was closer to my own whistle. It was exciting to be able to do something I never could on earth.

I thought back to my interview with Jesus.

You said I was made to do good in the world in my lifetime. All my life, I wanted to make people happy. You might call that a gift, but I say it's a curse. When you realize how much evil there is in the world, but you can't do anything to change it, well, that's just too much.

"Tell me about it!"

It was his voice in my head. I was sure of it. Was Jesus listening? Reading my mind?

I continued.

Even my own mother told me I should be patient with Claire because it was easier for me to be good than for Claire. What a crock! We're different, that's for sure, but neither of us has it easier because of our differences.

"Your mother may have been wrong."

He was reading my thoughts, but it didn't really bother me. Maybe he'd give me the answers to some of the questions I had been worried about for so long.

I think I felt happier in my little garden than I had ever felt on earth—even as a little girl on Christmas. Jesus had told me to take some time to enjoy myself before deciding what I wanted to do in heaven. He sounded like a therapist when he said that I needed to live some of my own personal dreams before I tried to jump right in and do good for others. If I managed to realize some of my own dreams, I would know more about myself and would mature in my understanding of things.

"There she is!" a man with an English accent said.

I looked up and saw two older men coming toward me. They were both in their fifties or sixties, and they were smiling and pointing at me.

Is one of these old geezers going to be my guide? I asked Jesus in my thoughts. I was disappointed. *I was thinking in terms of someone closer to my age.*

"Age doesn't have any meaning in heaven, Iris," he said.

CHAPTER 3

Introductions

"Hello, Iris," the one with the English accent said as he shook my hand. "Christian here just had to come along and see the niece he never met."

The other one also offered his hand, and I shook it.

"Come to think of it, I never met you either," the first one continued. "You have so much of your father and mother in you that it's obvious who you are. I'm your uncle, Gerald Anson. I'm to be your guide here in heaven. Have you ever heard of me?"

I looked him over and had my own thoughts about him. He reminded me of Santa Claus. He didn't have a beard or anything, but he had the twinkling eyes, red face, red nose, and white hair. He was pretty chubby, and his whole face was built around his smile. So Santa Claus. He was wearing a dark suit, a white shirt, and a dark tie. I remember thinking how conservative he looked. His suit pants had been neatly mended at the right knee. That's how I knew for sure it was Uncle Gerald. He had had polio as a kid and had worn a brace on his leg for the rest of his life. Aunt Vicky, Papa's sister, probably had to mend his pants all the time. I also noticed he didn't limp. Maybe you lose your earthly handicaps in heaven. Like my depression.

"I've met Aunt Vicky and all your children," I said. "We're all good friends."

Onkel Christian, Papa's brother, was bald (like all the men on Papa's side). His blue eyes twinkled mischievously, and his olive skin was not what I would've expected from a typical German. (Mom told me she thought he looked like Marlon Brando when he was young.) Papa looks more German than that, but he does tan easily. Both uncles were a little shorter than me. Onkel Christian had his arm around my shoulder and told me how glad he was to meet me.

Should I hug them? I wondered for only a second. I suddenly was filled with love for these old men. I hugged them both and felt an inner warmth from their love. Warm fuzzies.

Uncle Gerald said, "When I heard that you were coming—and here I was, ready to take on a new ward—I asked for the privilege of being your guide. Heaven, you'll find out, is a pretty marvelous place. You can imagine anything you want to see and do anything you want to do. You set the parameters—difficult or easy—and the Lord does the rest. I'm sure you've noticed that already in the creation of this lovely garden. It will continue to develop to suit you until you decide to leave it as it is. I think it's rather lovely already. I wouldn't change a thing."

"Perhaps a few calla lilies over here?" Onkel Christian suggested in a heavy German accent.

"*In Ordnung!*" I said, and the beautiful creamy white flowers appeared in full bloom.

Onkel Christian beamed when he heard me speak German. I had learned quite a bit while visiting the relatives, but I had never felt fluent. Now, it seemed I could hold a complete conversation in Papa's native language.

Maybe I should call it my father tongue. Oh, man, that's lame, but it's still pretty funny. It felt unbelievably good to be able to have a funny thought. I hugged both uncles again and was filled with warm fuzzies once more. I started to think I might like being in heaven after all.

"Duh!" said Jesus in my head.

"I usually start by introducing newcomers to their relatives here. You can get your bearings at the same time. You'll discover that you have special powers in heaven, and we'll develop these as we go along," Uncle Gerald explained as we walked toward a dirt road that wasn't there before.

Heaven is a lot like earth in many ways. There are forests, cities, farms, stores, and playgrounds— anything you could ask for—but there are some very important differences. First of all, you only do what you want to do. That's the reward for having been good on earth and doing all the stuff you didn't really want to do. Second, everything is peaceful. There's no fighting and no wars. I guess, if everyone can have whatever they want—and they don't bother anyone else with it—there's no reason for wars. It's kind of unreal, but neat. On the other hand, it made me think that this might be just a dream. Could I be in a hospital, in a coma, or something?

As we walked along, Uncle Gerald pointed out some lions sitting beside lambs.

"I always wondered about that while on earth," he said. "I make sure to show it to every new soul in my care. Since no one has to eat in heaven, there's no drive to kill. Lions who aren't hungry don't have to kill. Of course, an occasional lion likes to hone his skills, but that's all part of his creative activity—an illusion of sorts—and doesn't harm any animals. In fact, a gazelle might want to practice its own techniques of evasion using the same method of illusion."

That seemed weird to me. Why should they even want to play prey or predator? But then again, Sara used to run around my apartment all the time. I thought it was exercise, but maybe it was really honing her skills. I wondered if the big-game hunters who came to heaven did the same kind of thing. I sure wouldn't like to see that!

"What was your impression of the Lord?" Uncle Gerald asked.

What can I say? He was everything I would have expected, I guess. He was perfect. I'm kind of sorry I had those fits of anger.

"He knew everything about me, and he still loved me. He wanted me to be happy," I said.

"How did he appear to you? I mean, I was judged by God the Father when I arrived."

"Oh. I saw Jesus, but I wonder who the non-Christians see," I said.

"I believe people see the image of God with which they are the most familiar. I always pictured God as an old man with white hair, a long white beard, and a white robe. I wasn't disappointed. Others have seen him sitting on a throne, and still others have seen the dove. It's all the same God, just different representations of him, based on the person's own thoughts about how he should look."

So I'm kind of confused. You might change your looks, but how do you appear to different people at the same time? Jesus didn't have anything to say this time. Maybe he didn't want to reveal his secrets. At the same time, I had to wonder again if all this might be a dream.

"Why did he refer to himself as 'we'? Is it because of the Father, Son, and Holy Spirit?" Again, I pictured the three of them sitting around a conference table and agreeing to give me the shortcut to heaven. Not a good picture.

"I suspect the Three Persons use the majestic plural. That's the plural used by kings and the pope to refer to themselves," Uncle Gerald explained.

That made sense. After all, God is greater than kings and the pope. On the other hand, why should he feel the need?

"Yes, well, that's what *I* think," Uncle Gerald said. "But there's a lot of discussion about this here in the first level of heaven."

"First level!" I exclaimed. "I never knew there were levels in heaven." Of course not. I didn't believe in heaven.

"Of course. This is where you begin to make the adjustment to the spirit world. If you ended up in seventh heaven right away, you'd go through severe culture shock. This place looks like earth, but it's all illusory. This is where you learn about yourself as a spirit. And believe me, going through the levels slowly is best. This takes patience, but it allows you to grow spiritually in a more solid way. When it comes time for you to serve, you'll be better prepared to do your job right. Don't rush yourself. You have all eternity ahead of you."

I wondered what I'd have to learn in each level. And I wondered how they'd be different. I also wondered what exactly spiritual growth meant. It sounded suspiciously like school. Maybe heaven was more like earth than I thought.

"Have you given any thought to what you'd like to do in heaven, Iris?" Uncle Gerald asked.

"Do you mean, like, a job?"

"That would come later. I mean, what is your pleasure?"

"Oh. Actually, I'd like to continue learning to play the guitar and maybe a few other instruments. And if I could, I'd like to visit some places I didn't get to see on earth."

"Will you start with music then?" Uncle Gerald didn't wait for an answer. "What kind of music do you like?"

"There isn't any music I don't like, but I know you and Onkel Christian like jazz, so that would do for now. It's what I was working on when I, er, left the earth." (I couldn't put myself and *died* in the same sentence. The word just stuck in my throat.)

"All right then." Uncle Gerald was rubbing his hands together, eager to get started. "First, the relatives. After that, I'll take you to where all the musicians congregate. Christian will come along too, won't you?"

Onkel Christian said, "Absolutely! I love listening to all those jazz greats."

We crested a hill, and I saw a large group of people rushing toward us.

"Oh my goodness!" I yelled. "They look just like the pictures on the wall at home."

Opa looked a lot like Papa: tall, bald, blue eyes. He was even bowlegged. Oma had had a major stroke after Papa's birth, but she wasn't limping in heaven. It looked like you did lose your physical defects in heaven. She actually looked strong and healthy.

Onkel Christian looked really happy to see his family. We switched to German. I guess people are most comfortable with their own native language, but Uncle Gerald didn't have any trouble talking with them in German. There was a guy standing next to Opa. Onkel Christian introduced him as Onkel Artur, Opa's brother. They had a bunch of sisters, but Karl and Artur were the only boys in the family, so they were always close. The two of them looked just like in the painting by Onkel Artur, standing together with cigars in their hands and fedoras on their heads. They were a little scary, actually, but Oma looked nice. She was happy to see Onkel Christian, her oldest. I also met our ancestor, Johann Paul von Wassenau, the forester. I wondered if I could visit his seventeenth-century world. It would be cool, even if it were only illusory.

I hugged them all and almost felt like I had known them all my life. Oma took me in her arms and made me feel extra special. I could feel the warmth of her love filling me through and through. Warm fuzzies again. I tried not to giggle, but I couldn't help myself.

Uncle Gerald approached me after a while and told me it was time to go. "You can return here anytime you want, just by wishing for it. The other relatives have been waiting to meet you, too."

I said "Auf Wiedersehen" to everyone, gave hugs all around one more time, and followed Uncle Gerald down the road.

"We're walking today so that you can gradually adjust to how things are done here. I've found that people adjust better if we do things slowly. Over the next rise, you'll meet some of your mother's relatives. Since they speak French most of the time, they don't do much with the Irish relatives, but I wanted you to meet them first because most of them play some sort of musical instrument. You'll meet the Irish ones right after. Your great aunt Anne-Marie, who just recently joined us, may be able to help you get acquainted. She's quite an accomplished musician herself. And now that she has shed some of those earthly handicaps, she can play any instrument she wants. Of course, being old and a romantic, she likes the harp best. But I'll wager she changes after she loses more of her human prejudices. Here she is."

I had forgotten that Aunt Anne-Marie had died just a couple of months before. I looked at her and couldn't believe she was the same person. She had been schizophrenic for most of her life and had been the kind of person who looked like she knew she didn't fit in. She used to shift her weight from one foot to the other and was sort of always moving her hands, as if she didn't know where to put them. But now, she was different. You could call her radiant, if that didn't sound so lame. Her smile was for real, and she looked totally happy.

"Come try this piano out, Iris."

She remembered my name. I was impressed. I sat down at her piano and played Pachelbel's "Canon in D" perfectly, better than I ever had in my life. It was amazing.

"You can get a piano for yourself, just by wishing for it," Aunt Anne-Marie said exuberantly. "Or a harp." She sat down at her harp, pulled it expertly toward her, and played me a whimsical tune.

I could understand why she liked the harp. It sounded so mystically magical. It was really good to see her so happy. She lived for more than eighty years as a misfit on earth. I could tell she liked being in heaven: she could do what she wanted, no one judged her, and she didn't need drugs that made her someone she wasn't. Wow! It was the same with me. I hated that drugged-up feeling. She must've had it a lot worse. Maybe I *was* lucky to have gotten the shortcut after all. No, probably not. I had had a plan to get over my problems.

I looked around and saw that all our relatives were watching us and smiling. We were their two newest members. After a while, I asked my great-grandmother (I called her Grand-Mère), in almost perfect French, to play the accordion for me. Mr. Fisher should've heard my French. I was pretty good, not like in high school. Grand-Mère played the accordion perfectly, just like Mom said. Then she gave Grand-Père a look, stomped her foot, and started on a quadrille. I panicked as Grand-Père came toward me, obviously intending to dance with me.

The quadrille is a fast dance with complicated steps, but Grand-Père whispered in my ear, "Just wish for it," and everything went fine. It was a lot of fun, especially when everybody else joined in.

If I can learn to play instruments this quickly in heaven, I may run out of things to learn.

"No way, Jose!" Jesus was back in my thoughts.

After the dance, I saw a really cute guy coming toward Grand-Père and me. He had dark hair, brown eyes, and a friendly smile, and he was just a little older than me. Most of the other relatives were—let's face it—ancient.

"Hi, Iris. My name's Ray. Your grandparents used to visit my family in Saint Pete, and I know some of your aunts and uncles. I think we're, like, second cousins, once removed. How does that sound?" His eyes were gentle. "Could I join you guys for a while?" he asked.

"I kind of like the idea. Let's see what my uncle says."

Uncle Gerald was okay with it, and I was happy to have a younger man join us.

It was time to continue down the road and meet the Irish relatives. I wished all the others "Au revoir" and promised to return soon for piano and accordion lessons—and maybe even harp lessons.

In no time at all, we were with the Irish relatives. Someone was playing a honky-tonk piano.

"That's Rita," a boy said.

I turned and saw two good-looking boys, who were about sixteen years old, standing together. They had an Irish look about them: dark hair, pale skin, and blue eyes.

"They're your mum's cousins, Johnny and Chucky. They died in their teens," Uncle Gerald explained. "They had muscular dystrophy and spent years in wheelchairs. They're inseparable. Now that they don't have the handicap of their bodies, what do you think they want to do to serve the Lord? They're in training to become archangels. They're anxious to fight for what's right. You won't catch me doing anything like that. That's something for idealistic young men. Johnny and Chucky? This is Iris."

"Right. Jeanne's daughter. Hi, Iris. How are you?" one of the boys asked.

"Fine. But which of you is which?"

"I'm Chucky," the taller, more slender one answered.

"And I'm Johnny," said the broader, stronger-looking one.

"Which of you is older?"

Johnny and Chucky gave each other a knowing glance.

"Why does everyone ask that?" Johnny sounded annoyed.

Chucky answered my question. "Technically, Johnny's older because he was born a year before me. But I was sixteen at death and Johnny was fifteen. It doesn't really matter in heaven though. Everyone here is truly equal, and no one needs to be treated like a child."

I thought it might get interesting when their younger brother Timmy got to heaven. "I met your brother, you know. He has four kids: two boys and two girls."

"Yup. Dad told us. And our baby sister Maddy has two girls," Chucky announced.

Oops. I forgot Uncle Chuck had died recently too. He was so cool. He let us cover him with the bows and ribbons at Mémère and Grandpa's fortieth anniversary. We were such dorks. I asked them where he was.

"Are you kidding? He's out doing all the things he didn't get to do while he was in the world. I bet he didn't realize you'd be here today. He keeps telling everyone how nice Jeanne's kids are, especially Iris," Johnny said with a wink.

I could tell I was blushing. Now I'd have to live up to Uncle Chuck's words.

Jesus interrupted my thoughts. "He told the truth. Why shouldn't you be a nice person?"

Jesus, are you reading my thoughts again? I hope no one else can.

"No. Just us."

Phew!

"And you guys are going to be archangels?" I asked, changing the subject. "Why?"

Chucky explained, "All our lives, we wanted to do all the normal things boys get to do. We hardly even had a chance to play Cowboys and Indians because we were in wheelchairs before we were old enough to be trusted with sticks. We would sit in the living room and watch TV all day. Sometimes, we had tutors come in, but basically, we had nothing to do. So we talked about all the things we would do when we were healed. Of course, there was no cure for muscular dystrophy in our time—there still isn't—so we were only healed when we reached heaven. Now we want to live the adventure. Plus, it's a chance to show our gratitude to God for making life on earth so short, relative to eternity."

I liked these guys. They were going to make great archangels. But Archangel Chucky?

"You may have to take new names," I said.

"I'm going to be Archangel Charles," Chucky said.

"And I'm going to be Archangel Jacques, spelled J-a-c-q-u-e-s," Johnny said. "I really like that name, especially the spelling."

"Archangel Jacques. Cool."

There were still plenty of relatives to meet there, but Uncle Gerald was ready to go on. I introduced myself, hugged my mom's nana and grandpa, and promised to return soon.

CHAPTER 4

Babies in Heaven

"And now, the music," Uncle Gerald announced with a flair. His first task was finished, and it was time for fun. "What kind of guitar did you have in mind, Iris? John Denver just recently joined us, but I'm thinking he's more your mother's type. Then there's also Elvis."

I remembered John Denver. What a show he had with the Muppets. I wouldn't mind meeting him sometime, but there was someone else.

"How about Stevie Ray Vaughan?" I asked.

"As a matter of fact, he's available too. But would you also like some classical guitar? You know, I was quite a musician in my day. I taught saxophone, piano, guitar, violin…"

"Violin? I would love to learn to play violin!"

"Well, you're going to be one busy lady."

"I like being busy, it means I'm alive." Oops. Maybe that was the wrong thing to say.

Uncle Gerald didn't seem to notice. Maybe it was accepted as a figure of speech.

"So you like music, Iris?" Ray asked.

"Oh ya. Music is the greatest. I like all kinds— classical, jazz, blues, rock—maybe not country. That was about all there was on the radio when we lived in Louisiana. I got so I enjoyed it, but when we moved to Hawaii, and I got to the new school, it was really out, so then I hated it. Lately, I was working on getting good with the guitar so that I could enter a music therapy program. I had learned a lot, but it was hard work. I didn't have so much time for my friends, which I didn't like. That's when I was hit by a car."

Ray sure was easy to talk to.

As we walked along, Onkel Christian rejoined us. He was a jovial guy and told me all about my father's childhood and my parents' courtship. He was telling me things I had never heard before, and the nice part was that Uncle Gerald could add even more tidbits of information, even though he hadn't spoken German on earth. And Ray could also follow along just fine.

It reminded me of a movie I had seen when I was a kid, where all these space travelers—creatures from different worlds— wore little disks on their shirts to help them communicate. With the disks on, they could understand each other perfectly, even though each was speaking in his own language. Uncle Gerald and Onkel Christian understood each other perfectly, whether they were speaking English or German or a mix of the two, and I could talk with all my relatives in English, French, or German. It was pretty neat.

We were still walking along the dirt road in the countryside when a beautiful lady suddenly appeared before us. I knew right away it was Mary, Jesus's mother. She was beautiful, like you always hear, and the air all around us smelled like roses.

She was holding a tiny baby wrapped in a blue blanket. I thought it might be the Baby Jesus, but I didn't know. Maybe it was some other baby. Plenty of babies die, and they must go to heaven too. Maybe Mary takes care of them.

Uncle Gerald introduced us and then stepped off to the side with Onkel Christian and Ray to give us some privacy.

"Your mother has asked me in prayer to look after you in heaven," Mary said with a smile. "I see that you have a very competent guide in your uncle. He's one of our best, so I don't expect you to have any problems. If you do, simply wish for me to appear, and I will come. If I can't come right away, I'll send Catherine, your patroness. She'll be able to help you."

Her voice was like singing, and she was really nice. I could feel her comforting love as she talked. I wished I could tell Mom all about her.

"Thank you, Mary," I said. "So can I assume that my parents know I'm here and I'm safe?"

"Your parents were given the message of your uncle's vision, but their faith isn't always strong, so they waver. My Son, our Lord, is giving them every opportunity to grasp the fact that you are happily with us, but as I said, sometimes they believe, other times they don't. Don't worry, everything will work out in the end."

Mary changed the subject. "Tell me, what have you learned here, and what do you want to do?"

I told her about my meeting with Jesus, hinting that I wasn't in agreement about the shortcut idea. I described my garden to her, told her about my relatives, and that we were going to visit the musicians next.

"For now, Iris, take your time and enjoy yourself. Eternity is a very long time. If you try to enjoy each moment fully, you'll grow in the Spirit, and your life in heaven will be very fruitful," she said.

All eternity does sound like a very long time, but I may need that long to have all my questions answered and to do everything I want to do.

The Blessed Virgin disappeared as suddenly as she had appeared, and I was alone with my uncles and cousin again.

"Well, that doesn't happen very often," Uncle Gerald said, looking around.

Onkel Christian and Ray nodded in agreement.

"I thought she was too busy in Medjugorje to do special solicitations in heaven," the German uncle added.

"It just goes to show how special Iris is." Uncle Gerald's eyes twinkled as he patted me on the shoulder, and Onkel Christian nodded emphatically. That was embarrassing. I looked at him and was about to say something, but he was busy looking at the sky with an air of anticipation.

Suddenly, he exclaimed, "There they are! I knew they wouldn't be far behind the Blessed Mother!" He turned to me, saying, "They're her special wards, you know."

"Who are they?" I asked. I was already surrounded by a bunch of cute, flying babies, flapping their wings around my face and tugging at my hair.

"They're cherubim," Uncle Gerald explained. He was looking with special interest at each individual. "All children who die at an early age, as well as miscarried babies, become cherubim," he continued. "They bring a lot of joy in heaven because they have the energy of little children, and they are completely innocent. Also, there are a lot of them. Most people who die during childhood do so before the age of five, you know."

"Ah, there he is, the little lamb!" He pointed to a boy cherub with platinum hair, blue eyes, and rosy cheeks. He seemed to be pulling the others away from my head, which I appreciated. "Here's another cousin, my little Bumble. His given name is Gerald, but I think Bumble suits him so much better, don't you?"

Bumble? I wondered where he got that name. He seemed to be the leader of the group closest to us. They were all much smaller, kind of like newborn babies.

"The groups are often made up of families. For example, Victoria had a few miscarriages, and Bumble is their leader," Uncle Gerald explained.

Aunt Vicky is Papa's sister. I met her while Papa was stationed in Germany. We drove through France and took a ferry across the English Channel for Christmas one year. We were all adults then, and we had met most of the cousins while living in Hawaii, so we were all very comfortable together.

Uncle Gerald leaned over close to my ear and whispered so that the cherubim wouldn't hear, "We call the aborted ones miscarriages too. In a sense, that's what they really are, and we don't want to hurt their feelings. It's not their fault." And then louder, "Here, I'll introduce you to some of Bumble's little companions. This one's Nancy, that's Oliver over there, Nicholas here… This one here is my grandson Alfie." He wrapped his hands around one who was slightly bigger than the miscarried ones.

I wondered how he could tell them apart. They pretty much all looked just like Bumble, except smaller. And they didn't hold still. Bumble seemed okay. He wasn't like a two-year-old kid at all. He acted much more grown-up. He was gentle with the others as he pushed them away from my face.

"Don't be frightened, Iris," he said. "They won't hurt you. They're just a little over-exuberant." He turned and looked behind him. "Here come some more of your relatives."

Two girl cherubim, one much older than the other, and a boy joined the group. They didn't look a bit like Ansons. I tried to figure it out. The older girl must have died in childhood. She was even bigger than Bumble. The little girl and the boy looked like miscarried babies. All three had brown curly hair and brown eyes. They were probably from the French side of the family.

"More cousins, Iris," Uncle Gerald announced. "These are from your mother's side of the family. The older girl is Emily." Emily made a cute little curtsy when she heard her name. "And the little one is Carly. The little boy is your Uncle Stephen."

"Just call me Stephen, Iris," the tiny boy cherub said in a twinkly voice.

"Welcome, Iris," Carly said in her own twinkly voice. "How do you like heaven so far?"

"I've only been here a little while, but so far, it's great!"

"It's the only place I know, but I'm really happy here," Carly said. "I couldn't imagine anyplace better."

Good point. Everything in heaven is hunky-dory.

"Emily is Aunt Marguerite's great-granddaughter," Ray explained. "Sometimes, she spends time with her Mémère. Aunt Marguerite tries to spoil her, of course, but Emily can't be spoiled, can you?" He smiled lovingly at our little cousin. I could tell there was a bond between them.

Emily was wearing ballet slippers and a pink tutu. It looked kind of cute with her pink-tipped cherub's wings.

"Are you a ballerina, Emily?" I asked.

"I'm still learning. Ballet was something I couldn't do on earth, so I'm learning here in heaven." She made a graceful little pirouette in midair. "What do you plan on doing first, Iris?" she asked me.

"I'm going to learn music—any and every instrument I can. I hope to become an expert on guitar and then go on to other instruments."

"My Mémère is teaching me to play the piano right now. Do you want to join in?"

"Absolutely! I'll probably see you there the next time I go."

As suddenly as they had appeared, the cherubim were on their way again, calling, "Goodbye. Goodbye." I was reminded of the munchkins in the *Wizard of Oz*. They were so cute.

"They often accompany the Blessed Mother to her apparitions on earth," Uncle Gerald explained. "I'm really glad you didn't talk down to them. Even though they look like babies, they're complete individuals, and they are able to make adult decisions in their own right.

"Now, Iris, we can get to the musicians in the blink of an eye if we want to. I just want to give you all the time you need to adjust to being in heaven. The next time you go to see the relatives, it will take a lot less time. So while we're trudging along, let's try flying. We'll just go for a few feet off the ground at first. All you have to do is imagine yourself as light as a feather. Then let yourself go as you walk along."

With all the practice I'd had doing relaxation exercises, I knew it wouldn't be hard. I concentrated on relaxing my body as I walked, allowing my steps to get longer and longer. I started to push off a little with the foot in the back, and the next thing I knew, I was floating between steps. It was a little hard to keep my flying position. My body wanted to roll over onto my back, but I caught on pretty quickly. I looked at my uncles and Ray, who were totally amazed at how well I was doing.

"Iris, you are a natural," Uncle Gerald said.

"For sure!" Ray said. "It took me days."

That made me feel pretty good.

The four of us floated at a leisurely pace toward the area where musicians of every type congregate. Ray and I flew a little way ahead, while my uncles followed at a distance. We made small talk at first, getting better acquainted. I asked Ray how he died.

"I had a seizure in my sleep," he answered. "You can imagine what a surprise it was for my family. Me too."

"Yeah, I'm still pretty mad about dying, and I don't know anything about how my folks are taking it. I have trouble saying the word *death*. And I'm thinking about my two sisters and my brother, too."

"Two sisters and a brother? No kidding? I have two brothers and a sister," Ray said. "What a coincidence."

"Really," I agreed. "I don't ever remember meeting your family. Did you come to any of my grand-parents' anniversaries?"

"Oh ya! We went to Gainesville often. There was a big celebration at a lake cabin one time. There were tons of you kids playing around in the water."

"Yup. Mémère and Grandpa had sixteen grandkids. We were all there, but I don't remember seeing you."

"My sister came with her six or seven kids at the time. They were all still young and were playing with you guys in the water," Ray said. "My little brother and I mixed in with your uncles. We stayed away from the little kids."

CHAPTER 5

Battle of the Bands in the Sky

We arrived at the musicians' cafe. About a hundred tables were in the center of a large shady area. Perfect live oak trees shaded all the tables, and stages were positioned in a circle around them. The musicians were simultaneously playing their own music. For some reason, though, I only heard what each of them was playing when I looked at them. I closed my eyes, but even then, it wasn't cacophony. I would hear something and could picture the group in my head.

"Wow! It's like a giant battle of the bands!" I yelled in surprise. "Is that Beethoven over there at the piano?"

"Yup," Ray answered. "Do you like him?"

"I do. But I'm also thinking how nice it must be for him to hear what he's playing. I just *love* to hear my music. And it makes me play better, with more feeling. His heart must be singing while he plays."

Maybe that's part of the greater reward they always talk about on earth.

"I know what you're saying," Ray said. "I feel the same way when I play."

"Do you like music too?"

"Of course. Do you know anyone who doesn't?"

"Good point," I said. "What do you play?"

"My thing is the electric guitar," he answered. "I'm not too bad on it."

My uncles arrived and led us to the modern music section. They were already swaying and snapping their fingers to the beat of the jazzier tunes. All of a sudden, Stevie Ray Vaughan was on the stage in front of me. I almost fainted! He was *so* handsome in real life. (Or *was* this real life?) I couldn't speak or move. I just stared at my hero. He was within touching distance, playing and singing, seemingly just for me. When he was finished, he smiled at us.

"Who's this gorgeous lady, Gerald?" he asked.

"Stevie Ray Vaughan, I'd like you to meet my niece, Iris. She'd like to learn to play the guitar as well as you do. Do you think you could help her?"

"Absolutely! Let's hear you play, Iris." He handed me my own Gibson guitar—or one that looked just like it.

As I was starting to tune it, Uncle Gerald said, "Christian and I are going over there to listen to Count Basie. When you finish here, be sure to find one of us before leaving. Heaven is a big place, and it wouldn't do for you to get lost on your very first day. Okay?"

"Okay. Thanks, Uncle Gerald. And if I'm taking too long, just come and get me."

"Now, don't you worry about us. This is *your* day."

And with that, my uncles grooved their way over to the jazz band. It was a riot to watch them. Even their shoulders moved up and down with the beat.

"What about you, Ray?" I asked my cousin, who was rapidly becoming a friend.

"I'll just sit here for a while," he answered. "Maybe I can learn something, too."

I turned to face Stevie Ray Vaughan. Stevie Ray Vaughan! It was like a dream. First, I showed him what I knew. It came as no surprise that all those fingerings I had worked so hard on back on earth came out perfectly in heaven. That alone was special. And then Stevie Ray showed me some more complicated things, which I was able to pick up practically right away.

"You have some special talent, Iris," he said.

And you are a very special teacher: kind, gentle, and patient.

I said, "Thank you. I'm sure being in heaven is a big help. On earth, I would've had to work for hours just to begin doing stuff like this."

I still had trouble accepting compliments. I guess you don't lose all your weaknesses in heaven.

"It's true that things are easier in heaven, but you would still have to have an ear for it, and an innate desire to play well, in order to do as well as you do," Stevie Ray explained. "I'm sure you would've succeeded on earth as a musician. It might have taken longer, but your persistence would have won out. In music therapy, your personality and smiling face would've made more difference than the music anyway." He looked like he meant it.

Actually, that did feel good. My smile may have seemed a little reserved, but inside, I was bubbling over.

It wasn't long before we were jamming. I didn't know how long I had been there when I saw Uncle Gerald and Onkel Christian. We had just finished a particularly difficult set. They and Ray were standing and applauding. All three were beaming. When you're happy, your family's happy, I guess.

"Come again anytime, Iris, to learn more or just to jam," Stevie Ray said. "I've really enjoyed it."

Should I give him a hug?

"Thank you so much," I said and gave him a bear hug. I looked him in the eyes as I said, "I've always had a special feeling while playing music, but with you, it was even better."

I felt like I was going to explode!

"Shall we stay here a while and just soak in the tunes?" Uncle Gerald asked as we walked toward a table in the center of the area.

Could I ask for anything better?

"Let's go for it!" I answered.

The four of us sat at a table together and listened to the music. I took plenty of time to listen to the old masters. Handel was conducting a presentation of his "Water Music." I wondered what he'd say if I told him that Mom always played that when she planned to get the house cleaned. It was our Saturday morning wake-up call. That kind of ruined the music for us, I guess, but Mom always got a lot of energy from it, dancing around the house with a dust mop or broom. I smiled at the thought of my mom dancing with a broom, wearing old jeans and a stained T-shirt. There, in the musicians' cafe, even house-work didn't sound like such a bad thing.

"What?" Ray asked when he saw my smile.

"Happy memories," I answered. "Do you ever reminisce about your childhood?"

"All the time."

It was Ray's turn to smile.

I nodded toward John Denver. "Do you remember him?"

"Yeah. 'John Denver and the Muppets.'" We both laughed.

"Hmm, the mosquitoes aren't bad tonight," I prompted.

"Not bad?" Ray replied in a great imitation of Kermit. "They're delicious!"

"You know, he was my kind of guy," I said. "He loved nature and loved to share it with other people. And he even tried to make a difference with alternative energy. I wonder why he had to die so young." I looked to Ray for an answer.

"You have to pray for answers to questions like that, Iris," he told me. "They won't just come to you 'cause you're in heaven. Some stuff does just come into your head, but that's mostly stuff you would've known anyway, if you had thought about it long enough. The really deep stuff you have to work out with God. That's how you grow in the Spirit."

I decided to put that off until later. I looked around and saw Wagner conducting the "Dance of the Valkyries." How did I know it was the "Dance of the Valkyries"? It must be one of those things you just know. I had never really listened to Wagner's music, so I gave it a try. It was amazing! It went right through me. I wanted to do a pirouette in midair, just like little Emily, but wearing a suit of armor instead of a tutu.

About that time, I noticed a man sitting alone at a table and looking our way. He looked Hispanic or maybe Caribbean. I thought he looked like a dirty old man, hoping to pick up an innocent young girl. When our eyes met, he winked at me. Then he got up and walked over to our table. That was scary. Is this *really* heaven? I looked at my uncles and Ray. They seemed totally unconcerned. The "dirty old man" pulled up a chair and asked if he could join us. Yup, Hispanic. The others nodded. I should have been okay, but instead I was petrified.

He looked at me and said, "Hello, Iris." He took off his yacht captain's hat and sat down. "We have some people in common," he said. "My son-in-law is your uncle."

My uncle? We had Spanish-speaking friends, but none of our relatives spoke Spanish, and none was married to a Hispanic person. Certainly not Papa's brothers. They were married to Germans. Mom's brothers? Maybe Uncle Mike. Aunt Molly's mother spoke Spanish, but I had never thought of Aunt Molly as Hispanic.

"Are you Aunt Molly's father?" I asked hesitantly.

He smiled broadly and nodded. "My name is Miguel." He reached his hand out to me.

"It's nice to meet you," I said, smiling and taking his hand.

"Can you tell me about my little granddaughters?" he asked, leaning toward me with a strong handshake and an eager smile.

"Sydney and Hannah? They are really sweet and happy little girls. I just helped Sydney put one of her poems to music the other day. We sang it for the family. It was fun," I said. He probably wanted to hear more. "They have a really happy home life, you can tell. They're not spoiled or anything, just happy. It's obvious their parents truly love them."

"That Molly. I knew she would be a good mother," Miguel said with tears in his eyes.

"And Uncle Mike is a good father," I added with a touch of family pride. We kids all loved Uncle Mike.

"Miguel is Michael in Spanish, you know," the grandfather said, as if he meant, "Of course he's a good father, his name is

Michael, isn't it?" He returned to his table after a while, deep in thought and listening to his music.

After he left, I thought about how scared I had been when he came over. I wonder why I reacted like that. Just because he had dark skin? That was prejudice. Pretty bad. I had never thought of myself as prejudiced. I never thought I judged people by their looks. Dirty old man? I couldn't believe I had seen him like that. And in heaven! I wondered where that kind of prejudice came from? It was my first lesson about myself in heaven. Pretty sad.

I slowly turned my thoughts back to the cafe and focused on jazz. I listened to Count Basie, Louis Armstrong, Benny Goodman, Duke Ellington, and Charlie Parker. It was amazing that all these guys were dead—and I was listening to them live! It was also amazing that I was dead. I didn't feel dead. In fact, I felt very much alive. I compared notes with my uncles and Ray, who also loved jazz. After a while, Uncle Gerald picked up a trumpet and joined in with Count Basie's band. His solo was amazing! Count Basie turned out to be a very friendly guy. He asked if anyone else wanted to join in.

"Any room for a guitar?" I asked. I was so glad I had been forcing myself not to be shy and sit quietly by, wishing and wanting. There was never anything to be afraid of, and it always turned out to be worth it.

"Guitar is cool, young lady," the Count said. As I reached for my guitar, I noticed that Ray was coming too. He picked up an electric guitar, tuned it expertly, and stood next to me with a mischievous grin.

"You too?" I asked, and as we got into "One O'Clock Jump," I was amazed at how good he really was! When I wished for the slide I had made out of a bottleneck on earth, presto!

There it was on my finger! It was awesome to be playing with such great artists. I felt like I was in heaven. When we were finished playing, I told Ray how much I liked his music.

He said, "Well, I told you I dabbled a little when I was living."

"Dabbled, huh? Well, that's some super dabbling!" I said.

"Thanks." He smiled.

After a while, Uncle Gerald suggested we go into a nearby grove of trees and talk a little more about being in heaven. I practiced flying the short distance. I wanted to make progress as quickly as possible. Ray flew beside me. The uncles lagged behind. I think they were hoping we'd bond. Ray was older than me, but he was still younger than my uncles. We had a lot more in common.

Ray asked, "Where were you from on earth, Iris?"

"I guess you could say I was from Florida at the end, but we lived all over when I was growing up because my father is in the army. Really, Hawaii feels most like home," I answered. "That's where we lived the longest."

"Were you the one who was born premature?"

I nodded.

"You must be about the same age as my sister's oldest girl. Maybe you even met Sarah when she went to college in Gainesville."

"Did she work at one of those restaurants where you throw peanut shells on the floor?"

Ray smiled.

"I met her once with my grandparents, but we never had a chance to get to know each other. I wasn't taking college classes then." I had also been in deep depression at that time.

We reached the grove of trees and sat down on benches in the shade. A warm breeze rustled the leaves of the oaks, which I took the time to examine more closely.

"English oak," I said. I had learned a lot about trees in college.

"Gerald is a traditionalist," Onkel Christian said. "He likes what he grew up with."

"Now, Iris, what do you think of heaven?" Uncle Gerald asked.

"It's really great! I mean, I never thought about what it would be like. I remember a movie where it was described as boring, with everyone flying around playing harps and sitting on clouds, but it's not like that at all. I've enjoyed every moment—well, almost every moment—since I got here."

"What moments didn't you enjoy?"

"Mary said my parents were having trouble believing that I'm all right. I wish they could know how happy I am—and that we'll be together when they come here. I wish I could see them or talk to them or something."

"It's not easy to accept the death of a child," Uncle Gerald explained. I guess he was an expert on the subject. "Even if your parents have the consolation of knowing you're in heaven, they can't instantly stop wishing for you to be with them. Give it time, and trust in God. Everything will fall into place."

I still felt like everything had happened too fast. "I wish I could see them, just once."

"And what would that accomplish?"

Well, of course, they'd have to see me too. "Maybe I could just appear to them, having fun…in a dream," I suggested.

"Now, Iris, did anyone from heaven ever appear to you while you were on earth?" Uncle Gerald wasn't being testy or anything. He was really gentle.

"No, but—"

"There are no buts. It's a matter of faith and trust in the Lord for both you and your parents. If the Lord wants your parents to see you in a dream, he'll do it without your knowing it. The sooner you accept that, the better it'll be for you."

I got the feeling he had had trouble letting go, and it might have been hard for him to accept the truth.

"I should patiently wait to hear how my family is dealing with my death without even inquiring?" My voice kind of cracked on that last word.

Uncle Gerald put his arm around my shoulders and drew me to him. "You should wait, with hope and trust in the Lord, who makes all things right," he said gently.

I didn't know how I was going to do that, but I figured I'd have to try. *Jesus, you do understand that we were all really close on earth, right? Every time we moved, we only had each other to lean on. The thought of spending the rest of eternity—or at least until they all come to heaven—without my family is scary.*

"Trust us, Iris. We'll sustain you. Time will go by quickly. You'll see." Jesus's voice in my heart was only a little comforting.

CHAPTER 6

Bears Bears Bears

After teaching me the basics of being in heaven, especially traveling from one place to another, both in heaven, and from heaven to earth and back, Uncle Gerald let me go out on my own for a while. He promised to come whenever I called for him, but he recommended that I also make contact with my patroness, Catherine of Siena.

"Will you take on a new ward now?" Now that I understood all the possibilities of heaven, I was nervous about being left alone.

"Oh, no!" he answered. "There's still a lot more to show you. I'll just be lazing around until you need me again. I may even go to a pub." His eyes were twinkling at the idea of a pub.

My schedule in heaven could not be compared to anything on earth. There's no need to measure time in eternity and no way to do it either. I alternated between music lessons and visits to earth to see all the things I had wanted to see someday, but hadn't had time to visit. I could travel between heaven and earth and within heaven, simply by wishing to be there.

My basic lessons in flying turned out to be very useful because keeping your balance in wish travel is the hardest part. You could get completely turned around and find yourself standing on your head in the middle of a mud puddle—or worse! I prefer to land in a more dignified position, thank you very much. Ray had already visited a lot of places on earth, but he accompanied me on most of my adventures just the same.

"I appreciate God's creation a lot more now," he said. "I could look at it over and over and never get tired of it."

We started in Alaska. I was thrilled about my powers. "I'm so glad we can fly. The state is gorgeous from the air, and we can really cover a lot of territory pretty fast."

"Do you want to take the tour at Denali National Park?" Ray asked. "They do it in an old school bus, and the driver explains a lot. The road is closed to other cars because of the fragile tundra, and they don't let you get off, except at a few places. But it's okay. We can get off whenever we want, and we won't mess up the tundra."

"Sounds great!" I said.

I thought I might see someone I knew on the bus. I wouldn't be able talk to them, but it might be nice to see them. Once on the bus, I looked around at the other passengers, but I didn't recognize anyone. What was I thinking? There must be thousands of people from all over the world who visit Denali National Park. What are the chances that I'd see someone I knew on this particular trip? I looked across the aisle at Ray. He was casually looking out the window and listening to the tour guide. He didn't seem to care about the people on the bus. (We were both invisible to them, of course.)

"Can you see the grizzlies out there on the left of the bus?" the tour guide asked as he set his binoculars down. "There's a mama and her three cubs. They're kind of far away, but if you watch carefully, you can see them move."

I said, "Ray, let's get off and get a better look!" We sat in the grass on a little rise just above the bear family and watched the cubs tossing around and growling at each other, pretending to be fighting for their territory.

"I can't believe one of them is actually yellow. I thought they were all medium brown. Each of these cubs is a different shade."

"Yup, that's true," Ray said. "I remember that from my first trip here. It was a surprise for me, too."

The cubs started attacking the mother, who was lying on her back, paws in the air, lazily soaking up the sunshine. She let them know, with a wide swing of her huge paw, that that was unacceptable behavior.

"I was jealous when my family came here without me, but I'm sure they never got such a good look at the wildlife!" I was actually grinning.

"Why didn't you come with them?" Ray asked.

"Now that's a long, involved story," I started.

But we do have all eternity…

"It was during the summer before I started college. We were moving away from Hawaii, and I had made plans to spend the summer as a guide at the Girl Scout canoe base in Minnesota. Our family had always planned to go to Alaska on the way home from Hawaii, and that's what they did that summer. I guess my depression must have been showing signs even then because I told myself I couldn't go with the family since their new car only had room for five passengers. My mom told me that they would find room for me—even buy a seat for the back of the station wagon—if I wanted to change my plans. I convinced myself that she was just talking and that the family had already made my move out of the house a permanent thing."

"Really?" Ray asked.

"Anyway," I continued, ignoring his shocked expression, "I opted to stick with my plan to go to the canoe base. The family took their monumental drive through California and Western Canada to Alaska and then across Canada and down to Georgia. They did stop off at the canoe base, and we had a nice few days together, but I always wondered if they would really have found a place for me if I had insisted on going with them. I guess I'll never know, will I?"

"It seems kind of pointless to wonder what might have happened. Do you want to know how I see it?"

I didn't really want to know. I thought he'd say that I was dumb not to go. But I heard myself say, "I guess so."

"The way I see it, you made your decision and didn't call your mom on her offer, so the responsibility lies with you. You can't blame your family. And you can do all those things yourself now, anyway, in a much better way, so you should let it go."

I knew he was right, but I had trouble accepting the fact. "I wish I had talked to my parents more," I said. "I wish I could run into them on one of these trips."

"Sure," Ray said. "I've been there and done that myself, but I can tell you from experience that you won't see anyone you knew in your lifetime while you're visiting the earth. I think, maybe, there's too much danger of us changing the course of history or something if we get into earthly things."

"Maybe you're right, but it doesn't make it any easier. It would be nice to explain things to them a little."

"Iris, just try to be patient. The time until your family joins you in heaven will go by faster than you think. (I'm always amazed at how quickly it flies by.) And you'll be ready to show them around. You can even ask them some lingering questions at that time…if you still have them."

He hadn't seen his family, and he didn't seem to mind so much. Maybe I'd just have to get used to it. I had all eternity.

We returned to the tour bus just in time to have Mount McKinley pointed out to us in the distance. Its peak, as usual, was shrouded in clouds, so we got off the bus again, flew up above the clouds, and walked on the glacier, enjoying the majestic beauty of the mountain. I've always enjoyed windy days, and the wind atop this mountain was more than exhilarating.

"I think the wind personifies the power of God," Ray yelled over its roar.

We really had to struggle to walk against it. Being spirits, we didn't have to feel the cold. (Thank God!) And we could even control the strength of the wind against us, so we were both able to enjoy exactly the experience we liked best. I love to have the wind stinging my face and blowing my hair straight back behind me, like a horse's mane and tail when it's running. After a while, Ray sat down on the glacier and watched me.

Whenever I've flown in a plane, I was always tempted to jump out the window and walk in the clouds. (I know you can't do that, but I was still tempted.) They look a lot like snow, and I figured you could walk on them like they were fresh snow. The top of Mount McKinley was above the clouds, so I gave it a try. It ended up being a huge disappointment. It was more like walking through wet, cold steam. Disgusting!

I looked over at Ray in the sun and thought about how patient he was being with me. He had already seen and experienced all this. Maybe he had been lonely in heaven, not having people his own age to be with. As we flew back to the bus, I asked him.

"I was never lonely before you came," he told me. "When I saw you, I thought we might get along for a while, so I asked if I could join you. I'm glad I did. I really like our talks. You're not only a beautiful woman, you're also very intelligent."

I was starting to enjoy compliments. I didn't even mind that I was blushing. I really trusted Ray.

Even though we didn't need to sleep and could travel at night, we usually sat and talked somewhere pleasant until sunrise—when we weren't returning to heaven for music lessons or other activities. Ray told me about his life on earth and his experiences in heaven, and I told him about my life. He was very understanding about my depression.

He summarized it like this: "You were born with a strong desire to make others happy. That's unusual. Most people are born selfish and have to learn the joy of caring about others. Naturally, you were confused by other people. You probably couldn't imagine how anyone would want to hurt another person. And you wanted others to want to make you happy, like you wanted to make them happy. But this made you feel guilty. You wanted to be kind and generous because it made you feel good, but you wondered if that was selfish because you enjoyed the praise that came with doing good deeds. Am I right?"

"It's like you can read my mind! I enjoyed the praise I got, but I don't think I did good deeds for praise. One time, my mother told me it was a great consolation to her to know that a person can be born with a strong desire to make others happy, not for praise, but just because it's the right thing to do. She said I was like that and it was a gift. I guess it was, but it was kind of hard to live with. I could actually feel other people's pain. It was as if I were the one suffering. I felt bad for everybody who was hurting and wanted to help them all. I saw everything that was wrong with the world and wanted to change it all. So many other people didn't seem to care. So I became depressed."

"Do you understand things better now?"

"After I came to heaven, I could understand everything a lot better. At first, I couldn't put any of my understanding into words, but I had some strong feelings. Now, I can put some things into words, but there are still some things that I can't explain. I know a lot of it has to do with our God-given free will. We have the right to choose between doing what's right and doing what isn't, but I can't understand why God would give free will to such imperfect creatures in the first place."

Ray laughed. "Now, I think that is a sensible question."

I wondered how much free will I actually had if I always instinctively felt compelled to do what was right and felt guilty whenever I didn't.

After Alaska, I showed Ray the huge canoeing wilderness area on the border between Minnesota and Canada. I had worked there every summer during my college years, guiding Girl Scouts on canoe trips. We used to paddle across pristine lakes, portage to other lakes, and camp in the wilderness. We felt like pioneers, dipping our tin cups into the lakes whenever we wanted a drink.

When Ray and I arrived at Moose Lake, I had a strange feeling that I had never had before. I kept getting an uncomfortable feeling when I least expected it. At first, I thought it was because I had spent so much time there during my life, but that answer didn't feel right. I asked Ray about it, but he didn't have any answers. Finally, I summoned Uncle Gerald.

"I can't understand it. I get a weird feeling in this place. Is it because I spent so much time here when I was living?" I asked.

"That might be it, but I think it's something else. Come with me to that island at the far end of the lake."

We flew over the water to a little island that overlooked a good part of the lake. During all my years paddling there, I had never noticed it. It wasn't very big, but it was big enough to have a few small trees and some blueberries growing on it. I noticed an eagle sitting on a branch of the tallest tree. The eerie feeling was even stronger.

"Whatever it is, it's definitely here," I announced.

"Look at that little spot over there close to the water's edge." Uncle Gerald pointed to a sunny spot, where a person might sit and look out over the water.

There, exactly where I would have chosen to sit, stood a wooden box. My stuffed black bear was sitting on it! Beary had been with me for as long as I could remember. I had even repaired him a few times when the stuffing had fallen out, and his head was floppy because of it. He had been with me through-out my hospitalizations. I held him close to me like a little kid during those scary times. My eyes filled with bittersweet tears.

"Your sisters and brother made that box, with your grandfather's help. Your family put your ashes in it and came here to deposit them in your favorite place—very recently, I might add. Your friends were with them, and they all paddled here from the Girl Scout canoe base. There was some discussion about putting you and your box 'in garbage,' if you know what that means."

I smiled and wiped my nose on my sleeve. "It's the spot in the middle, where you can put cargo. Anyone riding there gets to do just that: ride. No paddling. I used to hate to be in garbage, and everyone knows that."

Uncle Gerald nodded. He understood.

"Well, they all decided to leave Beary here with you," he explained.

"This must've been hard for them."

I was sad for my family and friends. I looked at the beautifully finished box with Beary perched floppily on top. Olivia had decorated it with purple and yellow flowers in her *Bauernstil*. (*Bauernstil*, literally translated, means "farm style." The flowers Olivia made with long strokes of thick paint look like a country style of art.) I wouldn't have liked to leave *their* ashes behind. I just couldn't imagine. It must've been so hard for them.

"They love you very much and are happy that you're at peace. They know that your life on earth was less than happy, and they love you enough to do without your presence, if only you're happy. Are you happy, Iris?" Uncle Gerald asked.

"I'm even happier now, knowing that they're not mad at me because of my stupidity."

"Stupidity?"

"Yes, it was stupid of me to cross the street on red."

Uncle Gerald gave a big sigh and said, "Iris, everyone makes mistakes. No one's perfect. Do you think you were the first to cross a street on red? Your family has forgiven you—and so has God. It's time for you to forgive yourself. You're not the cause of all the unhappiness in the world, you know. The best thing you can do for yourself and your family is to find happiness here in heaven. Forget your mistakes and enjoy your adventures."

After a few minutes, I said, "You're right, Uncle Gerald. I guess that's just part of shedding my humanity. I'll do my best." I smiled at him. "Do you think I could take Beary with me?"

"Of course!" Uncle Gerald was smiling too.

I picked up Beary and rejoined Ray on the other bank. As I continued to show him around, paddling the canoe in the peaceful lake, I had a sense of peace that had eluded me until then. I didn't have to worry about my family; they would be okay. I gave Beary, who was perched between my legs, a little pat on the head, a gentle one so that he wouldn't fall over because of the missing stuffing, and I smiled up at the bright blue sky. I said, "Thanks," and a tear rolled down my cheek.

"Another step in your spiritual development?" Ray asked.

"You got it!" Warm fuzzies again, and I knew that they came from God's love.

We canoed throughout the wilderness area that included two national parks—one American and one Canadian—stopping at nightfall at the established campsites along the shoreline. I pointed out that there had always been campers who left the areas in a less than natural state, and we Girl Scouts would always choose a new place to spend the night, so that we could clean up the area a little. It was only natural for me to continue this effort with Ray's help. We removed foil and other nonbiodegradable stuff from the campsites and flew them to civilization, where we put them in trash cans, and we collected firewood for the next group of campers. It would've been easy to produce a leaf rake out of thin air for purposes of clearing the fire pit, but I preferred to show Ray how to fashion a broom out of a recently fallen branch from a pine tree. In a natural area, I believe it's best to do things naturally.

Sometimes, a bear family would come sniffing around, looking for tidbits left behind or the blueberries that grew in abundance along the shoreline, but we were never bothered. Our presence wasn't even sensed by the bears. We'd sit up on a tree branch, watch the animals feed, and talk.

"There were times when we had to chase bears away from the berries because we wanted them for breakfast," I told Ray. "We carried only the bare necessities—and the packs still weighed about a hundred pounds—so we liked to surprise the girls with blueberry pancakes for breakfast if we could. My mother thought we were living unnecessarily dangerously since the bears usually didn't want to leave. I told her, 'You have to let them know who's in charge!' You should've seen the look on her face." Just thinking of it made me laugh.

It seemed like we were kindred spirits or whatever it's called. We would discuss things about earth and about heaven, one of us sometimes enlightening the other, but mostly agreeing with each other's philosophies.

Ray said he was amazed at my insights, which was a little less embarrassing than it would've been when I was living on earth, and I appreciated his insight. Whatever Ray said made total sense. We were both happy that we had met in this new life.

CHAPTER 7

Memories

After the canoe wilderness, I went alone to the small college I had gone to in Vermont. I love the wide-open space of the northern part of the state. The center and south are very mountainous, but the north is made up of rolling hills and farmland. My alma mater managed a wood lot, which I was in charge of for one semester, and I enjoyed walking through the little forest once more. I listened to the few birds that hadn't flown south and assessed the health of the trees.

New students were all around me. They looked so young and inexperienced, walking around with their notebooks, looking at the trees, and collecting leaves, bark, and seeds. They were asking each other about the bits of debris in the leaf litter, wondering which trees they might have come from. If they could've seen and heard me, I would've been able to answer most of their questions. Maybe that would've been interfering with the living.

When I did that project in my first year, I really worked hard at putting together my scrapbook of specimens from all the trees. I kept going back to the forest, looking for specimens to add to it. Papa was really impressed when I brought it home at Christmas. After that, he considered me the expert and kept asking me questions about trees. And boy, did he have questions! I should've been thrilled about being able to tell him stuff, but I felt put out, on the spot, and made to perform. I guess I was a pretty insecure adolescent.

There were a lot of memories there, and I wondered how long it would be until I would see my old friends from my college days. I knew that even if I wandered into the administration building, I wouldn't see the former teachers and college administrators who had been so helpful back then. I wondered about the meaning of all-powerful when I thought about how God had to keep track of all the souls roaming the earth. How could he watch them all and make sure they didn't see anyone they once knew? I guess God has supernatural capabilities we can't understand.

I had been a big sister to a young girl in the town. They asked us early on to participate in the program, and I had missed my family so much over that summer that I decided to try it. By now, Diana must've been nearly grown up. On a whim, I walked past her house, but no one was home. It was nice to reminisce about the times when a young girl had looked up to me, trusted me, and loved me. I wondered how she had turned out and what she might be doing.

The campus hadn't changed much. The leaves were gorgeous, just as they had been when I got there for my first year. It was like something out of the Little House books. We learned how to slaughter chickens the first week, and it was exciting, in a weird sort of way, to see the Thanksgiving turkeys strutting around, waiting for their turn. Still, during

Laura Ingalls Wilder's time, that had been completely natural. I always thought I had been born a hundred years too late. Our modern life is so far from nature, and it made me worry about where the world was going.

It was really good to go to school there. I got to try all kinds of things that I wouldn't have tried at home. It helped me learn who I was and what I wanted to do with my life. I wonder what would have happened if the college had let me spend the winter under a lean-to in the wood lot, like I wanted to. I probably would've frozen something important off—like an ear or part of my nose. I'd look pretty funny with part of my nose gone.

Some people think I got depressed because I went to such a weird college. They're completely wrong. I found myself there. The fact that the depression got so bad at the end of my second year was pure coincidence. It might've been even worse if I had gone to a more traditional college.

I had wanted to get a job after finishing up my AA, to take off some of the stress of college and learn more about myself, but Papa and Mom insisted that I needed to finish a four-year degree so I could earn enough to take care of myself. They wanted to be sure I'd be okay if something went wrong (like, if a marriage didn't work out.) They meant well, but I think they were wrong in my case. *Is it okay to think of my parents as having been wrong?*

Jesus answered my question right away. "Yes, it most definitely is, but it wouldn't be right to blame anyone. Parents are no more perfect than anyone else."

Yes, but their children might be nervous about going against them. I was having a casual conversation—with God!

"True, but finding the middle ground is part of growing up. Both parties have to work at it."

But I wonder how things would have turned out. I could've insisted on staying out of school and getting a job for a while. I might've gotten rid of the depression then.

"The only reason for mulling things over that you can't change is to learn something from them. Otherwise, what's done is done, and it's time to go on."

I thought about that for a little while. Maybe I do spend too much time thinking about what might have been. I can't change anything. I'll try to concentrate on the good things. And thank you, Jesus.

I left Vermont to meet Ray in Hawaii, on Oahu's north shore. I had always wanted to surf while living in Hawaii. I actually tried it once or twice, but I had never experienced the thrill of standing on the surfboard and riding a wave. Ray had done some surfing in Florida, but the waves on Oahu's north shore are much bigger than on Florida's Gulf Coast. We had agreed to meet at Sunset Beach next.

I found him sitting under a palm tree not far from the edge of the water. The sun was shining, and the constant breeze kept the air comfortably warm. He taught me to surf, and I was amazed at how quickly I could learn. It was a lot easier than when I had tried surfing with my friends in high school. It wasn't as easy as learning a new musical instrument, though, and I thought Stevie Ray might have been right about my musical ability.

"What did you do while I was in Vermont?" I asked Ray as we floated on our boards, waiting for a promising wave.

"I was praying."

"You what?" I was astonished.

"You don't pray, do you?"

I never even thought about it.

"No, I don't," I answered. I had never really gotten into the habit. "I did pray when I was younger, but I haven't really done it for a long time. I thought I didn't believe in God, only in nature, so I didn't pray."

"And what do you believe in now?"

"Well, obviously, I know now that God exists. Deep down, I probably always did believe in him while on earth. Maybe I needed to believe in him, but I couldn't rationalize him, so I let myself believe that the Native American way was right. And when you think about it, they also believe in a creator. They just have another way of representing him."

"You once said that you'd like to help your family during this rough time, right?"

Ray's dark eyes were gentle and sincere.

"You mean, I could pray for them?" I had never thought about that. When people have done all they can in an impossible situation, they say, "All we can do is pray…" But prayer is maybe more useful than that.

"Didn't you ever pray to the saints to intercede for you when you were going to Catholic school?" Ray continued.

"Naturally, but I didn't really understand too much. The whole Catholic thing was a mystery to me."

I really never had understood about prayer. How could praying to a former human being help? I could see asking God for help, but how could a saint help someone?

"Has it occurred to you that you are now a saint?"

"What? What do you mean? Saints are proclaimed by the pope after they've been dead about a hundred years. Don't they have to perform miracles and all that?"

Saint Iris. Talk about absurd.

"Those are the saints you hear about on earth. People are sure they went to heaven because they were so unusually good. You're supposed to act like them so you can go to heaven too. But anyone who actually makes it to heaven is a saint. You and I are saints. Even if we weren't, we could still pray for whoever we wanted. I pray for my parents, my brothers and sister, their children and grandchildren, and so on. Sometimes, I get a message that someone I knew on earth needs prayers, and I pray for them. Prayers from saints really help people with their problems. You should try it."

I didn't remember any prayers.

"How should I pray?" I asked.

"It's really easy in heaven. Just shut off all distractions and talk to God. Let him know who needs his help and ask him to help them out."

"That's dumb. God knows who needs what. Why should I tell him what he already knows?"

"God likes to hear from his creation. I can't really explain it any better than that, but I promise you that things will be better for those you love if you ask God to help them with their needs."

I thought about that. Ray had been a real good friend, and I knew I could trust him. I decided to see what Uncle Gerald had to say about prayer when I saw him next.

From Sunset Beach, we could look up into the Kahuku Mountains.

"That's where the Girl Scout camp is. Would you like to see my secret meditating spot?" I asked.

We followed the gravel road up into the hills. I'll never forget that road with its gates that you had to stop and unlock.

You could let your car by, but then, you had to lock the gate again. It seemed to take so long. I had been a teenager back then, going to camp, sometimes as a camper with my troop, sometimes as a helper with younger girls, but always as a Girl Scout. I really loved it. I was glad we could fly, though. It would be a hot walk up the hill on the open road. Close to the entrance to the camp, I saw the white ironwood saplings.

"Ray, look at these," I called as I landed on the side of the road. "A few come up every year, but they don't seem to grow into big trees."

He ran the soft, silky needles through his fingers and said, "Nice. God's creation in action."

I looked at him.

He explained, "When God created the world, he allowed for mutation so things could adapt to climate and habitat changes that would be inevitable. Nature is constantly experimenting. If conditions are favorable, some mutations will survive and give rise to new species that will possibly be better able to live in the changed environment. Thus, life on earth continues. Pretty cool."

"Wow! Such logic. It makes total sense," I said.

Shortly after we entered the camp, I led Ray up a steep, narrow trail. There was a large washed-out area on the hill to our left, and we could see signs that troops had taken steps to curb the erosion. Adjacent to the eroded area, and on the right side of the trail, was my secret spot. I sat down at the edge of a small ravine, just like I used to. I had my back to the trail and my feet hanging down into the ravine. I signaled for Ray to sit beside me on the carpet of ironwood needles.

"Just listen," I whispered.

We listened to the soft island breeze whistling through the trees and the invisible songbirds, which were overwhelming in their songs. Every now and then, there was a loud crack, as if a tree were breaking. I explained that it was the sound of the treetops hitting against each other. I had often gone there as an older girl, sometimes with one of my friends, and we had listened quietly, content in the solitude and each other's friendship.

Ray spoke quietly, "Iris, would you mind if I came here sometimes and used your meditation spot myself? I haven't found anything as nice as this in all my travels. Would it be okay?"

"Sure, it's okay. It would never bother me if you came here. I always feel safe and peaceful with you. I guess I trust you."

I had to smile, and he smiled back. It was nice to think that we'd be friends for all eternity.

We returned to Sunset Beach for a few more runs with the waves. At first, we were both lost in our own thoughts, but we were soon enjoying the beautiful day with perfect surf on a tropical island. When we had had our fill of surfing, I took Ray to other places I had visited with my family on the islands.

CHAPTER 8

Volcanoes and Values

The next morning, as we watched the sun rise over Haleakala Crater, on the island of Maui, I told Ray the Hawaiian legend about Maui catching the sun and bringing it here for his mother, who needed it to dry her cloth made of bark.

"'Haleakala' means 'House of the Sun,'" I said. "Do you see how the crater wall has fallen away on the far side? And the way the sky and the clouds seem to be touching it? Don't you think it looks like the end of the world?"

"I can see where you could get that feeling," Ray said. "It's as if the clouds are slipping down into an abyss."

Before the sun could heat the sand on the inside of the crater, I led him down along the path. There were beautiful silver plants growing there. They had sword-like leaves and stuck them out defiantly, as if to show that it was a feat of daring to grow in such a harsh environment. The older leaves spread flat around the base of the plants. The silverswords reminded Ray of century plants, and the tall stalk of each flower added to that impression.

"This is the only place on earth where silverswords grow," I said. "They're very fragile. If you walk too close to them, you crush their roots, and they die. You have to stay at least three feet away. They're my favorites."

"God's creation again. He created something beautiful to grow even in this dry place," Ray said, looking around at the vast crater. "This whole place is beautiful! I love the different colors of the sand— reds, yellows, oranges. I'm really glad you showed it to me. It must have been nice to travel all over the world and live in so many different places. My dad was retired from the air force long before I was born. I never lived anywhere but Saint Pete."

"I don't have any idea what it's like to live in the same place for a long time, but I know that moving away from your friends every few years isn't easy. Your best friends become your brothers and sisters," I said. "I don't know if that's good."

Ray thought about that point for a few minutes.

"From my experience," he said, "most people lose contact with their childhood friends anyway. But the family is always there, if you want it. Good contacts in your family are probably an asset."

"Maybe you're right. I guess it's a trade-off. We met lots of different people and experienced life in lots of places. We got to see a lot of the world, and we got to live in Hawaii for eight years. My father says Hawaii is as close to paradise as you can get on earth."

"Do you agree?" Ray asked. "I mean, now that you know a little about paradise?"

"Well, it's not paradise, but it is one of the nicest places I've been to on earth. The islands are beautiful, and the climate is practically perfect. Maybe it used to come close to how people imagined heaven to be, originally, when only the Polynesians lived here. They had everything they needed, or even wanted, with a minimum of effort. That was pretty much paradise to them, I guess."

I looked around at the natural beauty of the crater. Life is completely different all over the islands now. If the missionaries hadn't come to Hawaii in the first place, the people might still be living that paradisiacal lifestyle. Instead, everybody has to work to make a living, driving to work early in the morning and not getting home until suppertime. No one can play in the waves and the sunshine all day like they used to. That doesn't seem right to me. I can't believe they call it progress.

"I wonder what the missionaries were thinking of when they came to the islands. If they had left the Hawaiians alone, they might still be living their peaceful lifestyle," I said angrily.

"Peaceful lifestyle? Weren't they fierce warriors?" Ray countered. "And anyway, if it hadn't been the missionaries, it would've been someone else." He paused. "And who's to say that the Hawaiians would've remained content with a simple lifestyle? Once they could see how things were in the rest of the world, they might have wished for some of that too."

"But what made the missionaries think they were doing the islanders a favor?"

"You know the answer to that. The missionaries believed the heathens couldn't go to heaven without being saved. Teaching them about God was doing them a big favor. And civilizing them was a big deal," Ray explained. "Anyway, that's better than taking everything they could from the land and leaving the people to fend for themselves afterward, like most colonists did."

"But the missionaries' kids grew up and started plantations here, using whatever cheap labor they could find. And on top of that, they brought diseases to the islands that the people couldn't deal with. Do you know that a huge percentage of the original Hawaiians died from *our* childhood diseases?"

"I do, but the missionaries surely didn't know they were endangering the islanders. And think about the differences between that paradisiacal lifestyle and the Western lifestyle. Americans and Europeans have traditionally lived in a climate that doesn't allow them to survive with a minimum of effort. It's not in their psyche to just laze around all day and pick a few coconuts when they feel hungry or thirsty. They have the need to store up for a rainy day—and a cold winter—like hamsters. Then they build a shelter for their stores. And pretty soon, they have to put a lock on the door because they don't want to have their stores stolen by the lazy people. It just mushrooms. They teach their children to hamster because they want them to survive. Rules and laws are passed, and so the story goes."

Ya, I know. Missionaries brought Western traditions and values to a people who were doing all right on their own. Those people were nearly decimated by Western diseases, and the ones who survived had to learn the Western work ethic. So the idyllic lifestyle ended.

"Do you think the missionaries were right to want to bring Christian values to the Polynesians?" I asked.

"There are worse values than Christian values," Ray retorted.

I had to think about that. *Are the Hawaiians living their lives according to Christ's teachings? A lot of the rich people who run the islands are descendants of the missionaries, but they seem to have forgotten about taking care of the poor. On the other hand, most Americans think of themselves as middle class—even those who are really poor and those who are really rich. Maybe these rich descendants of the missionaries feel the same way. Maybe they don't see themselves as rich. Maybe they're just being hamsters. Saving for the rainy day or for their children's futures. This sure is complicated. You can't just decide that one is good and another is bad. There are too many extenuating circumstances.*

"Right!" Jesus's answer came booming into my head. I was shaken into realization.

I shouldn't be judging, right?

"Now you're getting it."

After Haleakala, we visited the volcanoes on the Big Island. First, we went to Kilauea, one of the world's most active volcanoes. Kilauea's crater was very different from Haleakala's. The floor was black, shiny, and hard as tar, and there was a smaller crater within the huge one. As we walked along the floor of the caldera to Halemaumau, the smaller crater, the air was very hot. The sun heated the crater floor just like a city street in summer. There were small piles of black rocks along the way so people wouldn't get lost since the scenery was the same all around us.

I mentioned that it had been one of the training areas for the moon walkers.

"I can see that!" Ray said, looking around him.

Halemaumau was full of hot lava, boiling and steaming below us, and there was a strong smell of sulfur. After checking it out, we decided to fly into the sky to watch another vent, which was actively spewing red-hot lava. It was like a red waterfall, and droplets were falling on the sides of the flow.

They cooled into tiny teardrop-shaped rocks, which the Hawaiians call Pele's tears. (Pele is the goddess of the volcano.)

"The Hawaiians say you can't take any of the lava rocks away from here. Some people have taken chunks of lava or a handful of Pele's tears with them, but they had so much bad luck that they mailed the lava back to the park. Pele is very possessive of her lava."

"I like the idea that you can have visitors so close to an active volcano," Ray observed. "Look at this river of lava flowing down the hillside—and there are hundreds of tourists watching it along the sides."

"Yup. It moves really slow. You can watch its progress, and you still have plenty of time to get out of its way. It takes houses, farmland, forests, and even roads on its way. I've seen where a tree trunk has rotted out in a perfect circle in the old lava.

"There are all kinds of stories about Hawaiians who prayed to Pele to spare their homes, and the lava actually flowed around their houses, leaving the buildings unscathed. But I'm not sure that was really much of a blessing. All the land around the spared building was covered with fresh hard lava and wouldn't be good for farming for eons. I suppose it was just a kind of proof of the value of prayer for the people."

"Sometimes I wonder if God works together with mythological gods and goddesses to keep things peaceful among peoples of the earth," Ray said.

"But then, wouldn't the mythological gods and goddesses have to exist?" I asked.

"Food for thought," Ray said. "But remember that he is God of gods."

"I never thought of it that way. Well, we've got all eternity to figure that one out too, haven't we?" I smiled. *But it does say in the Bible, "There is no other."*

We flew to the ocean, where the lava was flowing off a low cliff at the water's edge. A huge cloud of steam was rising from the water where the lava hit the ocean.

"When we lived here, there was a big deal in the news when the lava finally reached the sea. This island is still growing, and there were questions about who owns the new real estate. The lava flow swallows up land in its path, but then deposits new land at the shore."

"God's creation in action again," Ray said with a grin.

"I guess you could say that. I guess God is recycling matter through the volcanoes. Each of the islands in this chain is volcanic, and there are other volcanoes under the surface of the ocean that may appear later."

Maybe the earth isn't in danger of being destroyed by man after all. Maybe God's plan is still working. The earth might look very different in a few thousand years, but it's going to survive us. Man can't destroy God's creation. That's a comfort.

"Good girl, Iris. You're a quick one!" Jesus said. "But don't worry too much about man's demise, *we* are still in charge."

I wish I had realized this on earth; I might not have gotten so depressed if I had known you were in charge.

"What you know now will help you in the future. We are just working to make the world a better place."

I wondered if it was all right to consider myself part of that *we*.

After Volcanoes National Park, we went to another place where I had camped as a Girl Scout. There was a great wilderness area on Kauai that could only be reached by a two-day hike or by zodiac. Riding over the waves in a zodiac full of tourists, Ray and I saw sea turtles swimming free in the ocean. We jumped out of the zodiac and swam with them, bobbing up and down in the waves. The water was very refreshing. It was nice to do something that tourists weren't allowed to do. It felt kind of like cheating.

Steep cliffs meet the shoreline there, and water-falls catapult into the blue-green ocean all along the way. We just had to let a waterfall give us a shower, washing away the sticky salt water. Finally, the zodiac reached the primitive campground at Kalalau. I knew there was an old hippie settlement in the mountains, and we flew around to locate it. It was still inhabited by the same people and their offspring. They seemed to be living the idyllic life, surrounded by nature and uninhibited by the distractions of modern, materialistic life. I always wondered what it would be like to live with people who had decided to drop out of society all those years ago. I made a mental note to return for a long stay.

Flying back along the Kalalau Trail to civilization was much easier than hiking had been when I was a Girl Scout. We passed groups of hikers going in both directions and watched their reactions to all the hardships of backpacking.

"I never did anything like that on earth," Ray said.

"I always enjoyed a challenge like that. I think my spirit of adventure was my claim to fame. It made me feel good to accomplish something that was physically difficult. I even spent a Thanksgiving weekend fasting alone in the woods. It really felt good."

"Thanksgiving? People must've thought you were nuts!"

"Maybe they did, and maybe I was, but I still felt good about it."

"Was it because you didn't have a place to go?" Ray asked.

"Actually, I did have a place to go, but I wanted to go home. And that was too far away for such a short visit. So I did my own thing."

"And you really enjoyed it?"

"It felt good, but I would've enjoyed turkey dinner with my family much more."

"So you felt sorry for yourself, went out in the woods, and suffered alone?"

Ray knew me better than I knew myself. I had never thought of it that way, but he did have a point.

"Maybe you're right. My feelings were very confused for a long time. I felt like my family, or my parents, were anxious for me to grow up and be on my own. I wanted to live my own life, but I didn't want to be excluded from the family."

We returned to heaven. I needed time to sort out my feelings about my life on earth, and Ray wanted to do something useful for the Lord. Before separating, we agreed to spend some time after Christmas walking the Appalachian Trail, which I had wanted to do someday.

CHAPTER 9

Catherine of Siena

I was doing very well with my music lessons. Aunt Anne-Marie had taught me to read music for the piano and play the harp. Emily and I had learned some duets and had become good friends. (It was hard to believe I could be good friends with a six-year-old kid.) Grand-Mère had taught me to play the accordion. Uncle Gerald was still working with me on the violin, which seemed a little harder, and Stevie Ray and I just enjoyed jamming together. He had already taught me everything he knew, and sometimes, we shared a new tune that one of us had composed. He liked my "Prozac Junkie."

I was always happy in heaven—happier than I had ever been on earth. I didn't even really miss my friends and family anymore. I just wondered sometimes how they were. I would have loved some contact with them, but I was beginning to understand that everything would be all right in the end. That gave me a deep feeling of peace and well-being.

I decided that it was time to get acquainted with my patroness, Saint Catherine of Siena. There had been a few times in school when research on patron saints was assigned. I had never found much information on Saint Iris, who supposedly lived in first-century Rome. Since my middle name is Catherine, I had chosen Catherine of Siena. I was impressed with her because she had insisted on living her life the way she wanted. In fourteenth-century Italy, that was a pretty big deal. She might've even fit in with the women's lib movement of the twentieth century. I knew her biography by heart:

Catherine Benincasa was born in Siena, Italy, on March 25, 1347. She was the youngest of twenty-five children, and the villa in which she grew up was always full of family members, some of whom were married and had children. She was such a happy little girl that her family nicknamed her Joy. She had her first vision when she was six years old. While walking home with an older brother, she suddenly stopped in the middle of the road and gazed up at the sky. She could see Jesus seated with Peter, Paul, and John. When her brother grabbed her by the arm and pulled, her vision ended abruptly, and the little girl started to cry. That vision changed Catherine, and she vowed to devote her life to God. She loved prayer and solitude, and when she was with other children, she tried to teach them about the joy of prayer.

When she was twelve, her mother encouraged her to take better care of herself. It was time for her to think about marriage. She tried to obey her mother and dress in the lavish styles of the age, but she wasn't comfortable with it. She finally announced that she would never get married. Her parents, not taking her seriously, continued to talk about finding her a husband. Catherine knew her lush, long hair was her best asset, so she cut it off in defiance. Her parents punished her by making her do the servants' chores. They also made sure she was never alone because they knew she enjoyed solitude. But she remained sweet and joyful and continued to say she would never marry. Finally, her father gave in.

She was given a small cell in the home, and she spent years praying alone, scourging herself, and fasting. She sometimes had celestial visions, but she also experienced terrible visions that made her think that God had abandoned her. She never gave up on him, though, and prayed constantly for his help. Finally, in 1366, when she was nineteen, Jesus appeared to her in her cell, with his mother and the heavenly host. Mary took Catherine's hand and held it out to her Son. He put a ring on it and declared her his betrothed. He told her she was ready to go out into the world and face any temptations. She joined the Dominican tertiaries, a group made up mostly of widows, and mingled with the people of Siena. She and her fellow Dominicans cared for the sick in the city's hospitals. She herself chose to care for those with the most repulsive diseases—those who might not otherwise get the care they needed.

A group of followers gathered around Catherine, following her example of patiently and lovingly caring for the sick and preparing them for death. Miracles became attributed to her, and her influence grew. In 1375, on a visit to Pisa, she received the five wounds of Christ called the stigmata. These, as well as Jesus's ring, were visible only to her throughout her lifetime.

Shortly after receiving the stigmata, she became involved in church politics. At that time, the pope was in Avignon, France, with an entourage of French clerics, something the Italians didn't like at all. There was talk of war. Catherine hated any thought of war, and she wrote letters, trying to bring the Holy See back to Rome. Her greatest accomplishment of all may have been convincing Pope Gregory XI to do just that. Unfortunately, the move caused a schism, or division, in her beloved church. She wrote letters constantly in her attempts to reunite it, but it was only reunited after her death.

Catherine wrote *The Dialogue of Saint Catherine*, which she said was an inspiration of the Holy Spirit. She dictated it to a secretary since she had never learned to read or write. Near the end of her life, she was invited to the Vatican to serve as an adviser to the pope, a position of great honor, especially for a woman of her day. There, she humbled the learned theologians with her wisdom. (I always thought of the twelve-year-old Jesus in the Temple when I read this part.)

Because of a lifetime of extreme asceticism and her distress about the schism, Catherine's health began to wane. When she died in 1380 at the age of thirty-three, the ring and stigmata on her body became visible to everyone. She was declared a saint in 1461.

I tried to be like Catherine of Siena, but as I grew older, I decided that this God I had learned about as a child didn't work. There was a lot wrong with the world. Even those who claimed to be doing God's will seemed to be doing wrong. The conflict between organized religion and what I thought was God's will was so strong in my mind that I gave up on Christianity altogether. I looked into other religions, and some made more sense to me. I was especially impressed by the Native American interpretations of creation and life in union with nature. I had been looking into Eastern traditions when I left the earth.

I summoned Saint Catherine. I was surprised when she appeared before me. I had seen pictures of her in her Dominican robes with the stigmata and the ring that Jesus had given her. She was, like in the pictures, a beautiful, petite, and relatively young woman. Somehow, though, she looked familiar, and I was sure I had seen her before.

Catherine said, "You're surprised. Is it because you didn't know that you've seen me before?"

"Where was it? I can't remember."

"I was at your side during the worst times of your illness. Did you forget that I nursed many people when I was in the world?"

"No, I knew that. But I don't remember when I saw you."

"Each time they gave you shock therapy, I sat beside you and held your hand until you woke up. I reminded you of who you were and where you were. Dressed as a cleaning lady, I found Beary under your bed after you left and made sure he was sent to you. And each time you were in the crisis stabilization unit, I sat by your side, praying for your recovery. I was even beside you in the street after that car hit you. Now do you remember?"

"Maybe…vaguely." I started to feel bad.

"Well, anyway, that doesn't matter anymore," Catherine said, putting her arm around me. "Now you're here with us, and you're even more lovely than you were on earth. Is there something I can help you with?"

"I'm not sure. I think I just want to get acquainted first," I answered.

"That's totally understandable," she said.

We only had a name to connect us, but we spent hours telling each other about our lives. We had had completely different experiences on earth, but that didn't matter much. I've always had a huge interest in history, so I was fascinated by Catherine's descriptions of everyday life in fourteenth-century

Italy. Catherine, for her part, was interested in all the conveniences of the twentieth century. She was particularly fascinated with machines that could do laundry and dishes and a freestanding cooking fire that would go on and off with the turn of a knob.

"So if you wanted to make a soup, you would just put a pot of water with bones to boil—without having to bring firewood in or build a fire—add the vegetables, and let it cook until done? How would you keep the fire from getting too hot or dying out?" she asked.

I had to smile. "Actually, if I wanted a pot of soup, I'd go to the grocery store and get a can or box of soup mix, and it would be ready in five or ten minutes. However, to answer your question, if you wanted to make a soup from scratch, the heat would be easily adjusted by the knob, and the fuel would be fed to the burner automatically."

I had always thought I would've been happier in Laura Ingalls Wilder's time, but talking to Catherine made me realize how much I'd have to do every day just to get by. I always enjoyed roughing it on camping trips and all, but every day? I don't know. I used to hate the idea of air conditioning and microwaves, but when I was living in Florida, I appreciated them, especially the AC. And I would've had to get up a lot earlier to cook breakfast on the stove. And Laura Ingalls Wilder could at least read books. Catherine never even learned to read. I guess she could do needlework to pass the time. *I* could never do needle-work without TV or music, though. I guess, since they never knew about those things, they probably didn't miss them. Still, maybe I *was* lucky to have been born in the twentieth century after all.

In Catherine's time, people didn't go to work in factories or offices. The nobles ran things, the craftsmen like Catherine's father provided stuff and services, and the lower classes led lives of work and drudgery. Girls, even if they came from rich families, were sheltered and mostly uneducated, and their destinies were routinely decided for them. Even their mothers didn't consider questioning the decisions made by husbands, fathers, sons, and brothers. Catherine's defiance must have been unheard of. She must have had a lot of courage—more than I ever had. That made her even more special.

In order to better compare the two centuries, we decided to spend some time together in a nineties-style home in the suburbs. Catherine explained that I couldn't time travel yet, so we'd have to put off spending time in fourteenth-century Siena for a while. (She hinted that I would have an opportunity to time travel at Christmas.) She was really excited to live in my time.

I set up a 1990s house in the suburbs of Minneapolis, explaining that I preferred to spend winter in the north, and Minnesota was always a happy place for me. I added all the modern conveniences to our suburban home—even though I still didn't approve of some of them. I wanted to make the experience as authentic as possible for my patroness from the fourteenth century. There was a lot to show Catherine, and both of us took the project on in an almost scientific manner. We set up a rotating schedule of chores and planned each day around what was needed to keep the household going. Of course, there were no children involved. I considered asking whether we could borrow some cherubim for our project, but I decided it wasn't really necessary. Besides, I doubted any of them would have been willing to pretend to be babies or school kids.

All the machines delighted Catherine. She could do laundry and dishes while completing other tasks in the house. Scrubbing sinks and toilets until they shone was exciting to her because she had never had a bathroom before.

"Everything is truly different in this household," she exclaimed. "This morning, I baked the bread, did the laundry, washed the dishes, and scrubbed the floors all at the same time! I used to have to scrub the stone floors when I was a girl, and that used to take all day! First, I would fetch water from the well. We were lucky to have a well in the courtyard of our villa." She paused, her eyes twinkling as she remembered a childhood event. "Oh, I have to tell you this one: One of my sisters talked Father into filling the fountain with wine for her wedding reception. It was lovely to see the guests filling their goblets with wine at the fountain!" After a little giggle, Catherine finished her explanation about her floor-scrubbing days. "Anyway, if we hadn't had our own well, I would have had to go to the one on the market square. I also had to use cold water. Who ever heard of heating water just to clean floors?" She laughed. "I can remember how red my hands would get in the winter. And floor scrubbing was done on your hands and knees with a scrub brush in those days. No mops for me!"

One evening, as we sat before the fireplace sipping hot chocolate, Catherine said, "Iris, would your society allow someone like me to stay in a small room at home and pray for guidance from the Lord?"

I was surprised by the question and tried to imagine what a day in the nineties would be like for a girl like Catherine.

"First of all, you would be required to go to school." Her face lit up at that. "Some children are homeschooled, but there are strict guidelines there too," I continued. "Parents who homeschool have to answer to some kind of authority about what they teach and how their children are progressing. In other words, you would have to be learning what is required of all children before you would be allowed to be in seclusion."

"So far, so good," she replied enthusiastically. "I would've loved to go to school as a child. Would I be allowed to read the Bible?"

"Yes. In fact, some people use the Bible as the main resource for their home schools. But your wish to be alone with God so much of the time probably would have never been understood. Even if your parents had allowed it, others might have questioned their judgment. People who are different aren't very well accepted in modern society."

"So if I had lived in your day, I might not have been understood or accepted? Is that right?" Catherine seemed a little disappointed.

"Exactly. People would have wondered how you could enjoy a life of prayer and seclusion instead of doing what other children do. Our age is much more secular than yours was. Visions of Jesus don't carry much weight. Your life would be relatively unproductive. You probably wouldn't have a following, and you wouldn't have any influence on everyday events."

"That's sad. Even my father was forced to admit that the hand of God was involved in my life. It's depressing to think that a possibly productive person could be suppressed simply because she's different."

"Yes. I guess every age has its problems and misunderstandings. It'll just take more time. I wonder if there will ever be a perfect world."

"I hope you know the answer to that question," Catherine said.

Almost as soon as Catherine said it, a light went on in my head. There can never be a perfect world because of human weakness. People will—and should—strive for a better world. That's their mission, sort of, but you can only find perfection in heaven.

"It must be so hard to continuously strive for perfection only to come to the realization that you can never achieve it," I said.

"You're the one to answer that question, too," Catherine said.

"You're right! I wanted to change everything. I let myself get down because there was just too much wrong with the world." I had to laugh at the realization. Now I understood!

Another time, when we were making homemade pasta together, just for the fun of it, I tried to explain to Catherine why I had chosen her as my patroness.

"I was always amazed at how you held out against your parents. You were what we would call strong-willed. I would have been afraid to do something like that."

She said, "You have to consider that I had Jesus on my side. Religion in my day was part of life, and Jesus was appearing to me. I had to come to the conclusion that he wanted me to dedicate my life to him. If I had married, a husband and family would have taken my time away from him. Despite the fact that we had a houseful of servants, my mother never had a moment to herself. The same went for my married sisters. It was an okay life for them— but not for me. Besides, the vanity of my day was in direct contradiction to what I believed about God and the afterlife. People in my day were becoming much more worldly, ignoring what the church taught about life on earth being just a preparation for a better one in heaven."

I hesitated with my next question, trying to think of a nice way to put it into words. "Catherine, didn't it bother you that the church was full of people who were trying to live the good life on earth and collect fortunes for themselves? I mean, in the fourteenth century, the church hierarchy was pretty corrupt, wasn't it?"

"It's true, Iris, but I have to say that all that didn't even interest me. When I was a girl, I tried to step out of that world of secularism that was pervading every aspect of life, including the clergy. When I returned to the world after my time of trial and seclusion, I was not really a young woman of twenty. My Lord had given me wisdom beyond my years. I understood that people's faults in the earthly life had little to do with my mission. I strived to bring about change that would benefit the most people in the long run. My work with the sick brought me a following that helped me save many souls for God. My efforts in church politics were intended to bring about the salvation of even more people. If people had seen division in the church, they would surely have given up on God altogether and never seen salvation. I worked to keep peace in the church. Criticizing her corrupt aspects would have probably made matters worse, don't you think?"

Catherine was truly wise.

"Do you think I'll ever learn enough to be useful to God?" I asked.

"I'm sure you will," she answered, and her face lit up with a bright smile. "After all, eternity is a long time."

CHAPTER 10

Period Differences

Catherine and I were beginning to realize that there were more differences between our former life-styles than similarities. Yet humanity had remained relatively the same. People in general still had to fight against greed—their own and that of others—but taken as individuals, the people of both centuries were essentially good.

"When I was living in seclusion, I knew there was a lot of evil in the world," Catherine said. "It took a lot of personal courage to go out into that world and reach out to those in need. I was pleasantly surprised to discover how many people were willing to follow my example. No one had the courage to start something they knew needed to be done, but once the action was started, people flocked to follow. I learned that most people want to be good, but if they don't have a good example to follow, they can also be evil. In general, they need a leader, and they need a leader they can be proud to follow. That's why it was important to let them spread the word of the miracles attributed to me."

"So in short, your seclusion helped build the strength of a leader for God, and your leadership was good for mankind?" It was a question but also a statement, and phrasing it made me compare my own life to Catherine's. "If I had had more confidence, could I have done some good in the world, too? Like, say, Mother Teresa?"

"Who's to say how your life would've turned out? Maybe you had already accomplished all that God had in mind for you, and it was just plain time for you to return to him. Anyway, it's counterproductive to talk about what might have been. Besides, as I said, most people are followers. If everyone were a leader, what do you think would happen?"

It took me a while to answer.

"Anarchy, I guess."

Talking to Catherine like that was really cool. She was wise beyond her years. (On the other hand, she was over six hundred years old. I had to smile at that thought, even though I knew that Catherine had been every bit as wise six hundred years ago.)

"Catherine," I hesitated with this new question.

Catherine waited patiently.

"You used to scourge yourself. What was the purpose of that?"

"In my day, people believed that man was incapable of good, that we were essentially evil beings, and that we could only be saved by the grace of God. We believed our bodies were holding us back from loving God to the fullest. I punished my body, the most human part of my existence, in order to make myself more worthy of salvation. It was a fairly common practice among the pious of my day."

"What do you think about the fact that I used to cut and burn myself? I felt unworthy. Was that in the same direction?"

"I'm sorry to say that in my day, people might have thought you were possessed by a demon. People scourged their bodies to give strength to their souls. They believed that life on earth was nothing, that their bodies were sources of evil. To have the courage to punish your body was considered saintly. But to cut and burn yourself without piety as your goal would be considered crazy. Do you see what I mean? Punishing your body to be more perfect before God was accepted, but God was nowhere in the picture for you. I think it even gave you a certain pleasure."

I nodded.

"You wouldn't have fared well in my day. They might have burned you at the stake as a witch."

"So you don't think it was the same?"

"No, and neither do you," Catherine answered gently. "Iris, you were very confused. There's no doubt about that. But what you did was never out of love for God. You were looking for peace from your depression. It can't be seen as the same."

I was looking at my hands. I think she knew how bad I felt because she quickly added, "But I'm sure you would've found your way if you had lived longer. You were still young, still learning about yourself. You would've found a meaning in life and would've pursued it, and then you would've found a place for God in your life. That's the way of the world."

I jerked my head up at those words. "What do you mean? There are lots of people in the world who never find a place for God. How can you say that that's the way of the world?"

"God's plan for the world is for people to find true happiness. Those who do find it discover that it doesn't rest in the things of the world. Those who don't find it aren't truly searching. They're not ready to give up the things of the world, so they don't really want true happiness. I've watched you long enough to know that you would've found it in your life. But now, that's no longer necessary, right?" Catherine put her arm around me and smiled warmly.

"Right," I said, and I actually felt all right. I did have one other question. "A lot of my friends are very good people, but they probably will never find a place for God in their lives. Does that mean they won't be happy?"

"Finding a place for God is like finding your place in creation. They may not know that they've found God, but having a love for your fellow man that trumps even the love of yourself is, in essence, finding God. I'm sure they'll find happiness."

It was getting to be time for Christmas. I had always loved Christmas—even though I hadn't always believed in the true meaning of the day—and I decided to decorate the house for the holiday. I brought in a potted Christmas tree to be decorated for the season and then planted somewhere where it could live out its life. I put decorations and lights on it, making it look like the one my family had always had when I was growing up. There was one decoration in particular that I made sure to put on it.

"Look, Catherine," I said to my friend. "This was always my favorite. My godmother sent it to us when I was a little girl, and I always loved it. My mother told me I could have it when I had my own home." I paused. "I guess one of my sisters or my brother will get it now. I don't need it anymore."

It was a ball with clear plastic over the front of it. Inside the ball, behind the plastic front, there was a little drummer boy with a lamb.

"Why the little boy with a drum?" Catherine asked. "Does that symbolize something special?"

"It's a Christmas song. The drummer boy has nothing to give the Baby, so he plays for him on his drum. I always liked it," I explained.

"Yes, I can see where showing your love, even if you don't have money, would be a good example for this time of year. Well, it certainly is beautiful," Catherine said, seeing the ornament in a new light.

Under the tree, I found a spot for the manger scene. I remembered how the family cats had always knocked the statues down and told Catherine about the first Christmas with our first cat.

"We had a fake tree, but Amber still tried to climb it. That was funny. And then, she used to play with the ornaments dangling from the lowest branches. It didn't take us long to learn not to put anything of value on the bottom branches."

I had another idea. "Catherine, I know that God is for everyone and everyone really worships the same God—even though some of us do it in different ways. Do you think we could have a menorah on the table? You know, to celebrate the Feast of Lights, which is also a special celebration of God's love."

"That sounds wonderful," Catherine said. "I imagine Jesus celebrated Hanukkah too, although I'm pretty sure it wasn't celebrated the same way in his day."

We put a menorah with eight candles on the dining room table, and during the Feast of Lights, we lit one candle each evening. We weren't sure about how else to celebrate the feast, so we read one chapter out of the books of Maccabees each evening while the candles burned. Catherine had a special gift of being able to choose an appropriate chapter for each day.

On the eighth day, with all the candles lit, we read about the original Feast of Lights, sang hymns, and gave each other hugs, feeling the warmth and love we felt for each other. (Warm fuzzies!)

The next day, Catherine announced, "Now, it's almost time to go to Bethlehem for the big Christmas celebration. As a newcomer to heaven, you're allowed to come and participate in the first Christmas. Are you interested?"

"You mean, I can travel back in time to the actual day Jesus was born?" I exclaimed. Who wouldn't be interested? "Yes!"

"Your uncle will accompany you. You can join the angel choir, roam the streets of Bethlehem, or talk to the shepherds—whatever you choose. I will be joining a group of virgins. We do this every year. The ladies are mostly from ancient Roman times, but I like them all a lot. If you'd like me to meet you there, I'd be happy to do that. I could introduce you to some of my friends. One is Lucy, your grandmother's patroness, and another is Iris."

I knew the story about Saint Lucy and her eyes. Mémère said she was grossed out when Grand-Mère gave her a statue of her patroness. She told her about Lucy having her eyes cut out as a type of torture, and the statue had Lucy carrying a little tray with two eyeballs on it. It might be nice to meet her in person. (I assumed her eyes would be back in their sockets.) At first, I was stoked at the idea of meeting Saint Iris and learning her story firsthand. But then, I thought the ladies might like to have their time to themselves. I'd have plenty of time (all eternity!) to get to know Iris after Christmas.

"If you're having fun with your friends, don't worry about me," I said. "Will Ray be going along too?"

"I don't think so," Catherine answered. "You have to have reached seventh heaven to go again after your first year."

"Are there really seven levels in heaven?" I asked.

Catherine smiled. "In heaven, everything is relative. You don't get promoted from one level to the next, like in school. And you don't have an agenda for each level. They really can't even be counted. The number seven signifies something final in a special sort of way. The highest level is referred to as the seventh, but all the levels overlap. Ray is taking his time, learning and developing slowly, so that when he reaches the highest level, he'll be better able to enjoy the ecstasy of it. You should learn from his example."

"I think I understand what you're saying. I'll try not to rush," I said.

CHAPTER 11

Old Bethlehem

Uncle Gerald suddenly showed up later that day, asking if I was ready to go to Bethlehem. Of course I was. He told me to hold his hand and not let go; there were likely to be crowds in the air.

"Now, Iris," he said, "I want you to relax and let yourself go."

Right away, I made myself relax. I could've fallen over if I had wanted to.

"This is done by newcomers every year," he continued in a calm voice. "Don't worry. We've never had a mishap. I'll guide you slowly and carefully."

Everything was whirling around us. I saw streaks of bright light in a black emptiness. Were those days—or years— flashing by? I would've been scared if Uncle Gerald hadn't been there. After what seemed like days of travel in this strange kind of light and darkness, I found myself suspended in a night sky. A choir of angels was singing, "Gloria in Excelsis Deo," and I saw a town built of stone in the distance. It was idyllic, and we took the time to take in the mood and atmosphere of the scene. (Also, I needed to catch my breath.)

While we were hovering close to Bethlehem, Onkel Christian joined us. He had his own new-comer by his side. Joan was very tall and had curly blonde hair. She seemed to be about the same age as my parents. I could tell that she was an American, so I asked her about her life on earth.

"I was living in Georgia when I was called home," she said with a sad look. "I had a husband and three children, grandchildren, even my first great-grandchild! I really miss my family, and I wonder how they're doing."

Understanding Joan's feelings of loss, I asked her how long she had been in heaven. (There was no way I would use the words *die* or *death*.)

"I died in July." Joan obviously had no trouble with those words.

"What have you been doing since you got to heaven?"

"I've spent a lot of time with my grandmother. I call her Nana. She looks really good, and it's nice to see her whenever I want. We've spent months cooking and baking up a storm," she said with a smile. "And I've been to all my favorite places on earth. It's been fun, really. I just haven't figured out why I can't watch my own loved ones. You know, that's what we talk about on earth when someone has passed away."

"I know. But you can pray for them," I said. I felt a little like an expert, having come to heaven a month earlier than her.

"Well, I'm not much for prayer…"

"Welcome to the club," I said with a grin. "But I intend to learn. I have family back on earth too, and I really want to pray for them. Maybe we could try it together."

"Let me think about that," she said. She didn't look convinced.

Our guides reminded us that this would be our only chance to see the newborn Christ Child for a long time, and we all rushed to the stable in Bethlehem. It had a natural glow, and there was something surreal about the whole scene. The Baby looked like any newborn I had ever seen. His head seemed a little big for the rest of his body. When his mother changed him, his arms and legs wiggled and thrashed. He cried like any other baby when he was hungry, but somehow, it was different than with any other baby. Maybe it was the serenity of the whole scene. Maybe it was the glow. Maybe it was because I knew the truth. I couldn't say why he seemed special, but I could see a difference.

I looked at Mary, and it seemed like so long ago since she had visited me in heaven with her little blue bundle. She was just as beautiful as I remembered. Joseph stood next to her, steadfast and true—an example for any husband.

I figured something out that night. The whole scene was extremely peaceful. It epitomized how I felt, deep down, after having come to heaven. It was a feeling of no obligations or worries and just doing whatever you want and knowing you'd understand what everything is all about someday. I knew the story of Jesus's life. I knew it would be far from peaceful, but the serenity of his birth foretold the ultimate peace that would be found by everyone who went to heaven. I couldn't understand why Jesus would have to suffer and die for mankind, but I felt like I would understand everything someday. For the moment, that gave me a kind of inner peace.

Mary looked at me. "Would you like to hold the Baby?"

I had been allowed to hold all my younger siblings as newborns, so I felt pretty confident about taking Jesus into my arms. It had to be a great honor to be selected. I guessed it might have been because I had never had a child of my own on earth. At any rate, holding and looking at this helpless little bundle, I felt a sense of warmth in my heart that I had never felt before. My whole inner being seemed to reach out to this Baby with a fullness of love that I could hardly contain. I didn't know if this was because it was Jesus in my arms or if it was because he had awakened a motherly instinct in me, but it was the nicest feeling I had ever experienced. When I stepped back into the crowd after returning Jesus to his mother, Joan took my hand.

"You looked like a natural mother," she said. "How did it feel?"

"It was wonderful!" I couldn't say anything else because I was so full of that feeling.

Joan said, "I can remember when my little ones were born. The first time you hold them is so special! You're just filled with loving tenderness."

I was only half-listening. I felt like I was in a cloud.

It was part of the miracle of heaven that as many people who wanted to could be present at this blessed event. The saints were allowed to stay as long as they wanted, and they were never in anyone else's way. I took the time to thank God in my heart, and no one bothered me. When I was ready, Uncle Gerald and I left the stable to tour the town of Bethlehem. There were crowds everywhere, and I remembered that was why Mary and Joseph had to spend the night in a stable.

I looked at the throngs of people. I could tell which ones were spirits and which ones were humans. It was like when

I first saw Aunt Anne-Marie in heaven. She looked like the same lady I had known on earth—but very different at the same time. That air of peace was in the faces of the saints. It was like the wonder on the faces of toddlers who are looking at something completely new and wonderful. There were no preoccupations, concerns, or cares. Only joy.

"Would you like to join the angel choir?" Uncle Gerald asked. "I know you have a beautiful voice, and I'd like to join in, too. What do you say?"

"As long as they give me the words..." I said.

We floated up to the night sky on the out-skirts of town where the choir was producing the most beautiful sounds I had ever heard. Uncle Gerald joined the tenor section, while I sang second soprano. It didn't take long for me to stop worrying about my own singing and start blending right in with the choir. We sang for a long time, and I had the feeling that I was no longer an individual. I felt like part of a larger unit of creation, almost like a cell in the body of a person. I was listening to the choir and adding my own part in an attempt to improve upon the whole. I knew deep down that it was good. I was becoming part of a greater thing. I was learning to grow spiritually, and it felt absolutely super.

Uncle Gerald interrupted this feeling when he reminded me that I should experience as much as possible this first time in Bethlehem—and that there were still the shepherds to see. I couldn't imagine how I could handle any more deeply moving experiences, but I followed along, half in a trance, until we reached the hillside where the shepherds were watching their sheep. There, from the top of the hill, I could tell that something special had happened in Bethlehem. Besides the huge unnatural-looking star shining over the town, there was a glow in the sky surrounding its silhouette. The shepherds must have sensed something unusual even before the angel appeared to them. Two of them were discussing what they should do next.

"Look, Ben and Asher went down there hours ago and still haven't returned. And you want to take a chance and go down, too?"

"It's a quiet night. You should be able to watch all the sheep by yourself, Saul. Maybe this baby is just so special that Ben and Asher forgot to return and relieve us. I don't want to miss the event. What if it's the Messiah that everyone's been talking about? We'll be able to tell our grandchildren all about it. I'll run, and I promise to return in time for you to go down, too."

We walked up to the two shepherds, and Uncle Gerald calmly announced in Hebrew (I guessed) that we would watch the sheep so they both could go down to the town.

"We've already been down there," Uncle Gerald said. "It really is a blessed event. Neither of you should miss it."

I tried not to look surprised when I saw myself in shepherd's robes with a shepherd's staff. I'm sure I looked like a young man. As we watched Saul and his companion walk down the hill toward Bethlehem, I couldn't understand why the shepherds had trusted us with the sheep. I also wondered how they had suddenly been able to see two spirits. It was one of those small miracles.

"I don't know the first thing about caring for sheep, Iris, but I know you do. I'll depend on you for advice," Uncle Gerald said as he sat down on a rock.

I shook myself back to reality. "It's not really very hard. You just make sure none of them stray away, watch for predators, and that's about it. How did you know I studied about sheep?"

"The Lord reveals to me what I need to know." He shrugged. "Apparently, he wanted us to relieve these shepherds. Can we just sit here and chat a little?"

Uncle Gerald reached down for the wineskin the shepherds had left behind and took a good swallow. He offered it to me. Wine wasn't my drink of choice, but I took a sip. It tasted all right.

"How did you like holding the Baby?" Uncle Gerald's eyes were twinkling again.

"It was the most wonderful feeling I have ever had in my life," I said. "Is that the motherly instinct? My mom told me about it once."

"I imagine so. Victoria told me about it," he answered. "You know, there must also be a fatherly instinct. I had it."

He smiled broadly, his eyes still twinkling.

He's just like Santa Claus, and it's Christmas!

"The Blessed Mother doesn't offer the Baby Jesus to just anyone. I'd say she has a special place in her heart for you," he added.

I was a little embarrassed. "I can't imagine why, but I'm glad I got to hold him."

"And the choir?"

"After I let myself go and joined in, I felt like I was part of a greater whole. It was like Iris, the individual, was important for the success of the total picture or something like that."

"I know what you mean. I had the same feeling the first time I came to Bethlehem."

I realized then that Uncle Gerald must have had a first time too—like all the saints. And he must have waited some time before he could return.

"What's the story with time travel? Why is it that you can only travel in time when you've reached seventh heaven?"

"Time travel is pretty sensitive business. You have to be sure not to interfere with history," he explained. "You have to have reached that level of selflessness and trust in God to be able to see what happens without trying to make a change. You have to have internalized that what happens on earth is really just a preparation for life in heaven. It's probably hard for you to understand right now.

"Anyway, an exception was made for the birth of Jesus, and saints have been allowed to come to Old Bethlehem for their first Christmas in heaven since before my time. Come to think of it, that's a lot better than what their families must be going through on earth."

"I didn't think about that. I imagine my family might feel funny having Christmas without me. Last year, Claire wasn't there, but we were able to call her, and we knew she was having a nice holiday. This would be different."

"It's all part of life on earth, you know." There was a tone of compassion in Uncle Gerald's voice. "They have to continue to cope with difficulties until it's their time to join us in heaven. As you progress, you'll understand much better, and it won't bother you so much."

I hoped that was true.

"Did you see your Aunt Anne-Marie in the choir? She was singing first soprano. She has a beautiful voice. I think she was enjoying it as much as you were."

"I forgot. This is her first year too. I should have looked for her."

"She got to hold the Baby, too."

"That's so nice. I bet she really liked that. She miscarried her only baby, you know. Sometimes, when she got away with not taking her meds, she would say she had a baby growing inside her."

The sheep were grazing peacefully on the hill-side. Every now and then, Uncle Gerald would take a sip from the wineskin. The angel choir could still be heard, and the town continued to glow against the backdrop of the star-studded sky.

The night was lasting longer than it should have. The sun should have come up hours before. I had sung with the choir for over an hour, for sure. I had been at the stable a long time and walked through the whole town.

"What time do you think it is?" I asked Uncle Gerald.

"Oh, about one o'clock," he answered and winked. "In heaven, time is different. Lots of things can happen in an earth's minute, and sometimes, almost nothing happens for an entire earth year. But you don't notice that in heaven. Things just go on, from one occurrence to the next. 'No big deal,' as you Americans say. Although it seems like we've been here quite a long time, it's really not much past midnight. We have plenty of time for you to take in the whole experience. Are you enjoying sitting here, watching the sheep, and talking with your old uncle?"

"I think it was good to take a break from all the deeply moving experiences. So yes, I like resting here with you," I said.

"Now, I have an important question for you, Iris," he said, becoming more serious. "While you were on earth, did you ever do or say anything to anyone that you felt badly about for the rest of your life?"

"Are you kidding? All the time!" I answered.

Uncle Gerald put up a hand. "I don't want to know about specific events, but I want to try to put things in perspective for you by telling you about something I did in my life, all right?"

"This could be interesting."

Although I'm not a gossip, I think *my* eyes were twinkling, just a little bit.

"Now, let me think. This was after I had already had infantile paralysis and couldn't walk well. Naturally, I was pretty angry about the change to my way of life. I was out playing with one of my chums and couldn't keep up because of my heavy brace and clumsy walk. It was a warm spring day, quite unusual for merry old England, but my grandmother would never have let me out to play after my illness on any other kind of day.

"We were playing hide-and-seek, and it seemed like I was always it because I couldn't get very far while Roger was counting to twenty-five. Understanding my problem, Roger offered to be it and gave me a real chance to hide by counting to one hundred! What a kindness from a seven-year-old boy. Unfortunately, I was much too out of sorts to appreciate his offer. I went to hide, of course, but in a place where I could hold out a stick and trip him as he walked by. I did it very skillfully for a cripple, I might add. Roger tumbled down and hit his elbow on a stone. The next thing I knew, he was running home, screaming, 'He made me break my arm! He made me break my arm!' Indeed, Roger's arm was broken. He spent the better part of that summer in a plaster cast."

"Oh no! That's awful!"

"Oh yes. It truly was. But that was not the worst of it. In my shame and because I hadn't yet learned the value of an apology, I never told him how sorry I was about what had happened. I became a recluse, staying indoors to avoid all the boys who were normal. Since I made no attempts to mingle, they didn't come looking for the cripple with the heavy brace.

I was left to my own devices and developed a secluded lifestyle in the protected environment of my home."

"But it ate away at you, didn't it?" I knew all about a biting conscience.

"Yes. I never forgot what I had done to Roger. Later, I heard he had gone to war with the RAF and had been shot down behind enemy lines. He had been killed in the fiery crash of his bomber. So you see, I never had a chance to apologize to him—even after I learned the value of apology."

"That's so sad."

"Well, I told you the story because it has a happy ending. When I came to heaven, years ago, do you know who my guide was?"

"Roger?"

"Indeed! He must have known that I had regretted my action all my life, and he requested me personally. I apologized immediately, and we've had a gay old time in heaven since then. It's ironic that the strong, healthy chap had to die in the war, and I was allowed—because I couldn't go to war—to marry a wonderful woman and have five children. In the end, his sacrifice was greater than mine."

"Is this story really true?" I asked.

"Every word!" he said.

"Wow! Do all stories have happy endings in heaven?"

"That, I suppose, is up to the individuals. But it seems to me that there's a greater potential because of a greater enlightenment. If you have some unconfessed transgressions eating away at you, you can look forward to seeing the concerned persons when they arrive in heaven. That should give you some consolation, it's done that for me. I'm still waiting for some people to arrive, including your father."

"I bet I know what you're talking about. Papa often tells the story about how you threw him out of your house once. He's not mad at you. He just says you lost it for a while."

"I'm happy to hear that he's not angry, but I'm not sure I like the idea about the whole world hearing the story." Uncle Gerald shifted his weight uncomfortably on the stony ground.

After a pause, I broached the subject that had been weighing on me for a few weeks. "Uncle Gerald, I'd like to pray for some people. Could you help me?"

"Of course. But I would have thought Catherine would have taught you quite a bit about praying already," Uncle Gerald answered.

"She did. But I haven't really developed a style of my own yet. Maybe you could give me a few pointers."

"Well, to start off with, prayers should begin with praise for God—"

"Does God really get something out of that?" I interrupted. "I mean, if he's all-knowing, he ought to know that we praise him, right?"

"No one can speak for God, but I can tell you that you'll get something out of it. It helps to put things in perspective. You are relatively helpless without God, and the more often you remind yourself of that, the better your appreciation of God will be."

"Okay, so we praise him first. I still don't quite understand why, but I guess I'll catch on later."

"Then, you make your requests and end with more praise. Let me give you an example: 'Our Father, Who art in heaven.'"

Oh, brother…

Jesus interrupted my thoughts. "Don't knock it, Iris. It's the perfect prayer. We put it together ourselves."

"Hallowed be Thy Name.
Thy kingdom come;
Thy will be done
On earth as it is in heaven.
Give us this day our daily bread
And forgive us our trespasses
As we forgive those who trespass against us
And lead us not into temptation,
But deliver us from evil.

For Thine is the kingdom and the power and the glory forever. Amen.

Do you see how the Lord's Prayer is perfect, Iris?"

"But when I recite it, I have trouble paying attention to the meanings of the words. Let's face it, a lot of people know it by heart and just recite it while thinking over their plans for the day. Don't you have that problem?"

"I used to, until I took each part of the prayer out of context and meditated about its deeper meaning for me at the time. Now, I do that every now and then, and it continues to have meaning—even when I recite it in a hurry. Thoughts run through the brain more quickly than spoken words, so I get a mental image of the deeper meaning whenever I recite the words. Of course, it doesn't cover every petition I have, so I add on a personal request, just before the 'For Thine is the kingdom' bit. Try it. I think you'll find that it's quite a good way to start praying."

I decided to give it a try. Uncle Gerald had never given me bad advice. I wanted to get right on it as soon as I got back to heaven. I had collected a bunch of requests already. I wanted to pray for Mom, Papa, Claire, Olivia, Bill, all my friends at the canoe base, and Joe in Florida. (I hoped he was taking care of Sara.)

The eastern horizon was just beginning to lighten when the shepherds returned. They were unbelievably grateful to us.

"You have no idea what a special feeling this gave us! This is surely a great night. We'll be able to tell the story to our children and grandchildren for a long time to come. Thank you both!"

We had to leave before the sun rose completely. We shook hands all around and said, "Shalom."

Without a further word, Uncle Gerald led me behind some bushes, where we wouldn't be seen, and started the process of returning to heaven.

CHAPTER 12

A Family Christmas

In heaven, we were all sharing our experiences with each other and talking about everything we had learned. It had been just as exciting for each new saint as it had been for me. I met Aunt Anne-Marie and compared notes with her about holding the Christ Child and singing in the angel choir. She described the whole thing completely differently from the way I felt, but she was just as excited as I was about it. It reminded me that everyone is different and experiences things in different ways.

I also ran into Joan in heaven. She was talking about the pie season and confessed that she had never been able to make pies. Her grandmother was going to teach her, now that she was back from Old Bethlehem, but Joan wasn't holding out any hope.

"I don't even think being in heaven will help," she said. She looked pretty desperate.

I had to laugh at this grown woman's lack of confidence in pie baking.

"My grandmother makes the best pies in the world, and sometimes they don't come out perfect," I said. "The main thing is that they taste great. My mom taught me how to patch a broken crust. If you want, I'll show you sometime. I haven't made many pies myself and never all alone, but I'll gladly share what my grandmother and mother taught me."

"Let me see how things go with Nana. Then we can get together, okay?" she said. "I also have some friendship cake for you to try."

I had gotten to know most of my relatives in heaven during my off-and-on visits and felt comfortable with each group. Now I got to sample all the traditional holiday treats available to each side of the family. I was already familiar with most of the German treats and found that I could eat as much marzipan as I wanted without feeling full. I had never tasted carp, so I tried some of that. Oma breaded and fried it in a special way, and it was delicious. She promised to teach me how to fix it next Christmas. (I had thought that any Christmas after this one would be really boring. Maybe it wouldn't be too boring after all.)

When I went to wish the Irish relatives a merry Christmas, I ate some more things that I was already familiar with: Irish bread with freshly churned butter (okay, so I never had freshly churned butter before), hot tea with milk and sugar, and buttery potato cakes. Johnny and Chucky were devouring these treats, which Nana brought to them as fast as they could eat them. There were also roast mutton chops, bangers (sausages I had once tasted in England), and rashers, which were thick slices of the best bacon I had ever tasted.

With the French Canadians, there was pork pie as the main course. There was also a huge pot of six *pâtes* (sounds like *sea pout*), a dish including layers of meat, onions, potatoes, and piecrust. I had never tasted it before, but I could tell that the hot, steamy dish of tasty, tender meat and vegetables in thick gravy would be perfect on a cold winter's day in the frozen north. I decided I'd have to come around next year and learn to make this dish too.

Sometimes, when I visited the relatives, people I hadn't met yet came to visit. I finally got to meet Aunt Claire (Mémère's sister and Aunt Sis's godmother). Since Aunt Sis is my godmother, Aunt Claire was sort of like a great-godmother to me, which I thought was special. It turned out that she was very busy in the service of the Lord. Posing as a nun, she often went back to earth to lead classes in how to set up the churches for the various services. She was also often able to get businesspeople to donate for renovations, flowers, and other needs of the various church communities. She didn't restrict her efforts to Catholic churches either.

"I was taught that there was only one true church. But I know that God is calling everyone to come in closer union with him. I see myself as a facilitator. If people choose to worship him in Protestant churches, in synagogues, or mosques, I do what I can for their physical and aesthetic comfort in the hope that they will grow closer to him. No one knows that I'm a spirit. I had this full head of white hair from early on, so people think I'm just an energetic, little old lady offering my assistance."

"Could I go back to earth and try to make a difference too?" I asked.

"If that's the way you choose to serve the Lord. Sometimes, he finds little chores for saints along the way, and that helps them to decide. Anyway, even if you tried one thing and later decided you wanted to do another, you'd have the option to change. You still have your free will here in heaven," she said with a smile. "Raymond is visiting while on Christmas break from a young people's center in New Orleans. Have you talked to him about that?"

"Ray? I guess I've been so busy eating treats that I didn't even think about him. He's supposed to come with me to the Appalachian Trail next."

"You're having a good time with him, aren't you?" she asked.

"He's like the older brother I never had. He's really helping me understand a lot of what's happening," I said.

"It seems to me that you've been given a good group of mentors to help you along. God may have a special plan for you." Aunt Claire looked over my shoulder then and said, "There's Raymond. I think he's looking for you. Enjoy yourself in heaven, Iris. You deserve it. I'll see you again." She gave me a hug.

"Hey, stranger. How did you like Old Bethlehem?"

I couldn't believe how familiar his voice was.

"It was the best Christmas ever!" I said. "I got to hold the Christ Child, sing in the choir, and even helped Uncle Gerald relieve some shepherds so they could go to the nativity!"

That was it in a nutshell, but no nutshell could ever contain all the emotion I felt.

"I remember when I went. That's when I made my major conversion. Until then, I was just mad about having died, going around with a cloud over my head, and making myself miserable. Let's face it: dying young is a bummer."

I nodded. It was true.

"But Christmas in Old Bethlehem was like nothing I had ever experienced in my life. I knew then what it meant to be truly loved by God, and I wanted to make myself worthy of that love."

"Well put. I like that," I said.

"So was it like that for you?"

"Not really. I think I already knew about that true love thing. This was more like nirvana or something. I felt like I had that intimate relationship with God, but at the same time, I felt like a very small but important cog in a great big wheel. Understand?"

"I do." Ray paused before going on. "Are you interested in another important task right now?"

"A job for the Lord? Already? What is it?"

I didn't think I was ready for anything more important than singing in a choir or something like that.

"Right now, I'm working at a young adult center in New Orleans," Ray started. "I do individual counseling and classes for older teens and people in their twenties. My clients are already in job-training sessions or are still in high school, and they're pretty stable. I just have to follow them and make sure they're making progress. I train them in life skills, anger control, coping with frustration, and all that. My next life skills class will be about filing income tax returns. That should incorporate some of the lessons learned in coping with frustration," he said with a grin. "I'd like you to come with me because there's a girl there who needs help. I know she cuts herself, but you can't see any of the cuts. I think you could help her out. How do you feel about that?"

Oh, man. This is a much bigger deal than an angel choir. Even if she wants to stop cutting herself, she can only do it with professional help. My two months in the program didn't cure me.

I thought about that last cut I made after cleaning and oiling my pocketknife.

"I don't think I can help her. What can I say? Does she even want to be cured? It's like an addiction, you know. She'll need a lot of support. Does she have any support?"

Ray put his hands up to stop me. "Iris, you're not the same person you were when you first came to heaven. You've really grown spiritually. Deep down, you understand God's plan much better now. Let me at least tell you about Melody."

I could tell it meant a lot to him. It couldn't hurt to listen.

"Okay. You can tell me about Melody, but I reserve the right to say no."

That assertion made me feel like I really had grown since coming to heaven. I used to feel pretty guilty when I had to say no to someone who needed me.

Melody had grown up in the projects as the oldest of three children. Her mother was a single mom who left school at the age of sixteen to have her baby and moved into an apartment of her own. She had intentionally gotten pregnant in order to get away from her mother and be able to live her own life. (At that time, young mothers were given apartments of their own in the projects.) Over the years, she had had two more children, who were mostly cared for by Melody.

Now eighteen, Melody decided she didn't want to follow in her mother's footsteps. She was determined not to raise her children in the projects. As far as Ray knew, she hadn't had any children and wasn't a drug user. She had been coming to the center for a couple of years and was about to finish high school. The staff at the center was helping her make plans to attend beauty school. Although she was finishing high school, she still needed to learn the discipline required to get herself to classes every day. And she needed some sense of stability. Then, Ray was sure, she would stop cutting herself.

I sighed. "You're talking about a long commitment here, Ray, and very little hope of success. Do you know that?"

I knew what I was talking about. I had been involved with the mentally ill in all kinds of hospital and group home situations. People who had grown up in difficult circumstances had poor social skills, and even if they managed to get jobs, they usually couldn't hold them down for any length of time. The failure became a reason not to try anymore, and even if they did try, the possibility of success was minute because of poor self-esteem and negative feelings about the world in general. This girl would need energetic, loving, full-time support and counseling to succeed.

"I know it won't be easy, but if God is with us on this, we should be able to make a change for the good." Ray was adamant. He seemed to think I had some sort of talent.

I didn't want to get involved with Melody, but Ray was my bosom buddy. I didn't want to say no the first time he asked me for something.

"This is pretty big. Can I think about it for a while?" I asked.

"Sure," Ray answered with his friendly smile. "You can let me know after our Appalachian Trail thing. One more thing: I can only stay until the middle of January. That might seem long to the kids at the center since I just started there last month, but I asked my boss to tell them my sister was in trouble. That could give you an opening to come back with me."

I opened my mouth to protest, but he added, "If you decide to."

Talk about pressure!

CHAPTER 13

Winter Trekking

We started our Appalachian trek right after Christmas at Mount Katahdin in Maine. The original plan had been to take two months to explore the trail, which meant that we would arrive in Georgia around the time when spring would be breaking out. (That is, if it turned out to be a short winter.) But all that was irrelevant now. Ray had to return to his job in New Orleans by mid-January.

The walk along the Appalachian Trail required concentration. The path was narrow, rocky, and covered with snow. We decided to use our power as spirits to hover over the path. This way, we could move more quickly and still get the visual experience. We followed the white swatches painted on the trees that marked the trail. If we came to a bald area covered with granite, the swatches would be painted on the rock. Those weren't visible most of the time because snow and ice covered the granite slabs. We had to fly ahead and find the next swatch on a tree.

"My mom and I were supposed to hike part of this trail last summer—for just a few days— in Georgia. My sisters were jealous that she hadn't invited them. I wonder if she hiked it anyway, maybe with one of them. I was happy that she had chosen me and that the others were jealous. Isn't that awful?"

"Not really." Ray shrugged. "They call it sibling rivalry."

"Did you have a lot of sibling rivalry when you were growing up?" I asked.

"Sort of." Ray was thinking back. "I was pretty much alone, with a sister and brother much older than I was." He smiled. "They were upset that I got away with so much. Then, my little brother was born, quite a bit younger, but I loved that kid. He was special."

"We were all pretty close in age," I said. "I was five-and-a-half when Bill was born. He's the youngest. Claire and Olivia are between us. All my life, I wanted to do something special with Mom, but it never happened. Either she was too busy or I had plans of my own. I guess that's normal, but I was really looking forward to the Appalachian trip. Now, it'll never happen. I feel like I really missed out."

"You must've had some time alone with your mom while you were growing up," Ray said.

"Ya, but somehow, it never seemed like enough. When I was depressed, she would come to see me wherever I was staying, but we never got down to any real conversations. Maybe she didn't know what to say to me. Do you know what I mean?"

"You think she was afraid of talking to you?" Ray asked.

"When I was depressed…" I said. "I always did believe she didn't love me as much as the others. Maybe it's because I was the oldest. I remember her saying once that, whenever she had a new baby, she had to turn away from the older child in order to take care of the baby. This was when she thought Bill was slow to mature because she hadn't been forced to turn away from him to take care of another baby. Maybe my problem was the reverse of that. I wasn't quite two when Claire was born, so I don't remember how things were before that, when I was the only child. Maybe, subconsciously, I felt rejected. Three times. Anyway, I always thought she didn't love me as much as the others.

"But after I got depressed, Mom did as much as she could for me. She must have loved me a lot to do the things she did. I was sure of that, but I couldn't help but compare and judge her as not caring enough."

"But you were depressed. You weren't really yourself," Ray pointed out.

"True, but don't you think I could've appreciated her efforts more?"

"Are you worried that she might have been hurt by your actions?"

Ray was starting to sound like a counselor, but for some reason, I didn't mind.

"That might be it," I admitted.

"Do you think she would've continued to help and support you if she had felt hurt?"

I would surely continue to help someone— even if they didn't appreciate me. I would hope that they would someday see the light. (I wonder if that's masochistic.) Mom would drop everything if one of her kids really needed her. She tried all kinds of things to get Bill straightened out in school. She didn't hesitate to put him in the boys' school, where the tuition was even higher than at our high school.

She did things for me too. When I had the ruptured appendix, she called Chipmunk to stay with the kids while she waited with me at the hospital. And she left them alone every night, with a rented movie and no direct supervision, just so she could spend the evenings with me in the hospital. And she took Bill out of his high school in Germany for a whole semester, just so they could be with me in Gainesville when I was depressed.

"Once, when I was in the CSU—the crisis stabilization unit—my mom told me there was no way a mother could turn her back on her child. She said that was part of the bond established at birth. Even if I killed someone, she said, she couldn't stop loving me. It was good to know that she felt that way. I guess she would've forgiven me. To answer your question, yes, she would definitely have stuck by me, even if I hurt her feelings."

We glided along in silence, enjoying the solitude of the trail. I was thinking over my relationship with my mother and with other family members. We had been close because of the frequent moves, and I had been able to talk to my sisters as friends. Bill, five years younger than me, was a different matter. He was twelve when I left for college, and I hardly ever came home after that, even in the summers. I was glad that I had some time alone with him a month or so before leaving the earth. I also spent a lot of time with Papa in the last few months. I regretted that I hadn't had more time with my mom. We had become like friends—on an equal footing—and it would've been nice to spend more time with her before leaving.

"I guess I'll get to spend more time with my mom when she comes to heaven," I said with a sigh of resignation, breaking the silence of the Maine woods.

"Hey! What's with that tone?" Ray asked as he threw a snowball at me. It hit me right in the face and was actually refreshing. My train of thought was broken, and I made a snowball of my own, aiming for the back of his head. Ray, relatively inexperienced in snow, was soon lying in it, with me giving him a good face washing. We were both laughing hysterically as we continued down the trail.

We had come down from the mountain and were in the Hundred-Mile Wilderness. At that rate, we wouldn't even make it to Mount Washington in New Hampshire, but we both agreed that it would be better to enjoy the experience slowly, rather than to rush ahead in the hope of covering more territory. (We did have all eternity.) The Appalachian Trail, even in winter, proved to be just the kind of wilderness challenge that I enjoyed. Ray seemed interested as well, so we spent the full three weeks in Maine. There were no worries about hypothermia, frostbite, or other cold hazards since we were spirits, and we were able to thoroughly enjoy the winter wonderland.

"It must be an unbelievable challenge to walk this trail with a full pack," I mused as we crossed a frozen lake. "With all these wetlands, you'd have to be sure to have your clothes in brand-new Ziplocs or you'd be spending most of your time drying them."

Ray stopped dead in his tracks and turned to look at me in amazement.

"Ziplocs, huh? Great idea!"

"Girl Scouts," I shrugged. "In Hawaii, we had a great outdoor leader who knew all the tricks. You wouldn't think you needed training in wet weather hazards in Hawaii, but it does rain a lot in the mountains—and there can be a chill at night in the winter. With little girls not used to cold, Ziplocs were highly recommended. Chipmunk used to say—Chipmunk was her camp name—that you could put a complete set of clothing in a gallon-sized Ziploc, one set for each day, and take that set down to the showers, with your towel and bathing supplies in another Ziploc, take your shower, put on your dry clean clothes, and put the dirty ones in the empty bag. Cool, right?"

"I think an adult might not be able to get a whole set of clothing into one Ziploc, but it sounds like a good idea. Maybe I'll get to try it someday. Thanks for the tip," Ray said.

"There are all kinds of tricks to keeping dry in wet weather, so don't try anything on your own without consulting the expert—that's me—okay?" I said jokingly. I had always been self-conscious about jokes that might be considered showing off, but this time, I was pretty comfortable with it. It wasn't showing off if it was a skill being shared for the benefit of someone else.

At the end of three weeks, we were just on the border to New Hampshire. We flew up to get a feel and glimpse of Mount Washington, the highest peak in the Northeast. It was absolutely frigid, with a gale-force wind. I knew it was one of the coldest spots on earth, and Ray readily agreed with me. It happened to be a clear day, and we sat in the sun in the lee of a building and enjoyed the majestic view before returning to heaven.

CHAPTER 14

Back on Earth

I decided to go back to New Orleans with Ray to try to help Melody. I could tell it was important to him. I was scared about maybe not being able to help her, but at the same time, I was a little tickled about the challenge. I was summoned before the Lord. This time, it was God the Father—in a white robe and a long white beard. His voice wasn't thunderous, as you might imagine. It was gentle but forceful. I had no desire to interrupt as he spoke.

"You have decided to look into the possibility of helping our daughter Melody, Iris. We're going to tell you what that entails. First of all, you will be given the imperfect body with which you passed from the natural world into the supernatural. This means that you will have all your scars, of course, but also, you will immediately sense the depression that plagued you for so long during your natural life. Don't be afraid: you have learned so much since coming to heaven that you will be able to overcome the depression in time. It will not be easy since it is a bodily depression and not a spiritual one, but you will manage just the same.

"We want you to spend the first few days in Raymond's apartment. You will be posing as his sister, which you are, according to our world order. We want you to work on controlling the depression. When you are ready to join Raymond in his work, you will go with him. Otherwise, you are not to leave his apartment alone. This is very important. Do you understand?"

"Yes, Lord," I said.

"You are very young among us to be venturing into the natural world. There is still very much for you to learn. We trust you to understand that your presence in the world of mortals could be catastrophic to them because you are so inexperienced. Raymond wants to save Melody, however, and we know that you can be helpful because of your great compassion. You must never lose sight of our greater goal, Iris. Even if you should not be able to help Melody at this time—even if she should die under your tutelage—you must realize that you cannot necessarily bring about change just because you want to. The forces of evil are very strong on earth at this time, and one solitary saint may not be able to win in a fight against them. If you give Melody just a ray of hope, you will be doing a great good."

God looked toward his feet, and I automatically followed his gaze. The clouds opened up, and we saw a typical American city below. There was a young lady in a public bathroom stall cutting herself in the abdomen with a razor blade. Her long dark hair was hanging down as she watched the blood flowing out of the cut. She was careful not to let any stain her clothes, and she let out a sigh of relief. I knew what was happening.

Scientists believe that flowing blood and excessive pain cause endorphins to be released in the brain. Endorphins are nature's tranquilizers. This process can reduce emotional pain, too. I looked more closely at the girl; tears were slowly rolling down her freckled cheeks. She was relaxed enough to cry. Melody had a lot of scars and a few fresh cuts on her belly, and I could see that she didn't know how to take care of them. Some were very inflamed. She had obviously never been a Girl Scout. She didn't seem to have a clue about first aid. Somebody would need to teach her how to take care of herself. That is, if she cared…

"Father, I want to help her, but I don't know if I can," I said.

"It's enough if you try. Perhaps meeting someone who has done the same and has survived will be enough for Melody. Be sure not to tell her too much of your own story. Just listen with your heart. I'll be there with you."

I noticed that he said *I*. Maybe that meant that this was especially important to him.

"I'll give it a try, Lord, because I know I can trust you, but please don't let me do anything that would make her worse. I don't think I could deal with that." I had to tell him the truth even though he knows all things.

"We have given human beings free will, Iris, which means that we will not make that promise. You will not be at fault if Melody chooses not to do what is right. We will be giving you the best advice there is. If you listen, you will have a chance at success."

And with that, the interview was over. I was nervous about this assignment. It was going to be a daunting task, I knew, but with God on my side, I felt confident that I had a chance to help Melody.

The next moment, I was in Ray's apartment in New Orleans. It was Friday, which was good, because I would need him to help me overcome the depression that was already setting in. I hoped that by Monday, I would be able to deal with it alone.

"I know what!" Ray was obviously trying to sound upbeat. "Let's go shopping! You'll need some cool clothes to wear."

I wondered if he could see the change in me and if he was regretting having asked me to come.

"Don't worry," he said, as if in answer to my thoughts. "God gave me a quick rundown of what to expect. He was sure you'd get over it in a few days. We just have to be sure you get plenty of rest. And no stress, okay?"

Rest? If only he knew. I used to have so much trouble sleeping. I wondered how much rest I'd actually get.

"Where do you want to go?" he asked, pulling out a very thick wallet.

"I usually shop at Goodwill," I said. "They have nice things for a good price."

"Goodwill? Are you serious? I have all this money," Ray said in pretend dismay.

"Used clothes will look more realistic anyway, Ray."

That made sense to him. "I don't know if there's a Goodwill around here, but there is a Salvation Army store up the street. Would that do?"

I had to smile. As if that would make a difference. "Of course!"

We headed out into the big city.

"Don't talk to anyone yet, Iris," Ray whispered as we walked down the street. "You don't want to have contact with anyone unnecessarily."

I couldn't imagine why a little hi might pose a problem, but I did as he said.

The Salvation Army store smelled a little musty, but it was neat and orderly. I picked out two pairs of loose-fitting jeans, a purple skirt, and a few T-shirts to try on, but Ray was rummaging through the nicer dresses.

"That's okay, Ray, I don't wear dresses very much," I explained. There was no need to waste his money on stuff I wouldn't need.

"Just one," he said. "For church."

"Oh ya." I hadn't been to church since high school. I wondered if I'd be able to take communion, now that I was a saint.

As I was trying on the clothes, I had the feeling I was being watched. The changing stall didn't have a door, and the back wall was a full-length mirror. I had my back to the opening, but the mirror showed my scars, of course. I turned and saw a girl about my age staring at my reflection. I covered myself in embarrassment but didn't say anything. The girl went on to another stall to try on her clothes. I should have taken a stall farther away from the entrance.

I met Ray outside the dressing room, and he held up a stylish dress in about my size, complete with matching shoes. I found a bra and slip that I thought might fit under the dress and returned to the dressing room. I took the same changing stall, inspired that it was the right thing to do. If more people knew that they weren't the only ones, they might have the courage to look for help. As I was fastening the bra, I had the same sensation that I was being watched. Turning around, I was surprised to see Melody standing in the doorway, staring at my scars.

Yikes! Now what? Don't smile, Iris. She doesn't know you know who she is. I should swear and tell her to get lost, but I'm not supposed to talk. Oh, man. Well, I'll just act embarrassed again and hope for the best.

Somewhere deep inside, I heard God say, "Well done, Iris!" Phew! I can count on God's voice even on earth.

The dress looked nice on me. It was blue with white raindrops and brought out the blue in my eyes. (They were crossing again, so I had to wear the glasses all the time.) The shoes were also blue. I'd never worn platform shoes and was afraid of my inherent clumsiness, but I decided to trust in the Lord. Of course, it may have been because I wanted to be a little bit cool. I smiled at my vanity.

"You'll need a purse too."

Ray dashed to the section of the store where the purses were on display. As luck would have it, there was one that matched the platform shoes perfectly— and it came with a matching wallet. I knew it could not be simple luck.

I looked up and whispered, "Thanks."

"Let's get you a lady's jacket—something you could wear with a dress or jeans," Ray said.

"I don't think that's necessary. I kind of like this one," I said, running my hands over the jacket Ray had lent me. It was brown corduroy with a knit collar. It was very warm and comfortable, and the wide corduroy was soft.

"You're kidding, right?" he said. "Let's just get you one of your own, okay?"

"If you say so." I sighed. Maybe we wouldn't have been bosom buddies on earth.

We found an appropriate camel-colored short coat and a matching set of dark brown hat and gloves. By then, I was totally reassured that God was watching our every move and making things happen for us.

Ray still wasn't ready to pay. "Now, about those shoes. They have to go, and you can't wear the plat-forms all the time. We'd better get you another pair."

I looked at my feet. I was wearing the purple Converse sneakers I had been wearing to the battle of the bands that night. They were really torn up. We both laughed. We went to the women's shoe section, but we didn't find anything that fit.

"I used to wear men's sneakers." I rushed toward the men's shoe section before he could say anything. There were quite a few good pairs of sneakers there, but I was feasting my eyes on a pair of leather army boots. They were just my size, and I decided I wanted them. "Would these be too weird?" I asked, holding them up.

"I guess they're in right now," Ray answered, his mouth a twisted smirk.

"What?" I demanded with a smile.

"Nothing. They're fine," he said, a little more cheerfully.

He was probably thinking they weren't very feminine—and they weren't—but he was humoring me, trying not to hurt my feelings.

"This is like Christmas," I said in a loud voice as we paid. Melody looked up at us from where she was looking over a rack of jeans. We both saw her. Ray smiled in her direction and nodded as the items were put into bags.

On our way back to Ray's apartment, I told him about my encounter with her in the dressing room.

"God works in mysterious ways," he said. "This way, when she meets you, she'll already know about your secret. You won't have to bring up the subject. It could be easier for you."

"That's if she recognizes me," I said.

"Just trust in the Lord," Ray said.

When we got to the apartment, it was lunch-time, and I was amazed at how hungry I was. In heaven, we only ate if and when we wanted to. It was a matter of pleasure. On earth, my body told me it was a matter of necessity. I opened the refrigerator, but Ray had been away for a few weeks. Almost everything in there was, as my sister Olivia would say, a science experiment.

"Do you have any money left, Ray?" I asked jokingly as I stood with the refrigerator door open.

Ray walked over and stood beside me. We both looked at what was inside and burst out laughing. It was so nice to be able to laugh, even with the depression. It was probably because of our friendship.

Ray went to the store while I cleaned the refrigerator. It was a very messy chore, and I couldn't believe I was doing it. At home, it used to take me days to get up the courage to face a job like that. At Ray's, I felt like I was doing something useful and constructive for my friend. Maybe Catherine was right when she said I would've been fine once I got over my own problems and had others to care about. Anyway, it seemed like the depression was already under control. Now that would be a miracle!

When Ray returned with his arms full of groceries, the refrigerator was spotless. We made ourselves sub sandwiches with potato chips and had Ben and Jerry's Chocolate Chip Cookie Dough ice cream for dessert. Ray had even bought Vlasic pickles. How did he know to get all my favorites?

"Guess what!" I said as we ate. "I think my depression is under control already."

"Oh? What makes you say that?" he asked.

"While I was cleaning the fridge, I remembered how I would've felt about that before. I wouldn't have done it in my own apartment. If I had been left at home to clean up a mess like that as a teenager, I would've felt like Cinderella. Today, I just did it— with almost no bad feelings—and it was done in no time at all!"

"You didn't think it was mean of me to leave you to clean up my mess while I went shopping?" he asked.

"Well, I sort of did think about that," I said with a slight smile and a sideways glance. "But the good part is that I got it done and felt good about it. I'm so happy now that I don't even remember how I felt at first."

"Would it ruin your good mood if I asked you to scrub the bathroom?" Ray asked tentatively.

"Do you want me to? I'm good at it—and quick," I replied instantly.

"No, no. Just kidding. I hope you can continue to control that depression though."

"Me too."

We spent the afternoon discussing Ray's strategy for Melody. I was to be Ray's sister, who was having emotional problems, and I was to be staying with Ray until I had myself straightened out. I would go with him to the center and would probably have a chance meeting with Melody. Without a particular job to tie up my time, I would be free to talk with her anytime.

On Sunday morning, we went to Mass. I had asked Ray about communion the night before.

"You went to Catholic schools all your life and never received communion?" he asked.

"My parents wanted us to get a good education, and Catholic schools were the best buy for your money. They sent us to them even though we weren't Catholic."

"I don't think going to communion matters too much, now that you've come to heaven, but you probably should follow the church rules while you're on earth and go through the training. It might be too late for this year since they start classes in the fall." He thought about that for a minute. "On the other hand, you did have religious education in your Catholic schools, right? They might make an exception for you. We'll ask Father Eugene tomorrow. For now, just ask for the blessing at communion time."

It was a sensible answer, but I was a little disappointed. There would never be enough time to go through the whole training period to become a Catholic. I thought I might never get a chance to receive. It might've seemed silly, but I had wanted to try it out when I was young—and I thought this would be a great opportunity.

Ray explained, "Since you're already a saint, you don't need to receive Holy Communion anyway. That's something for people who are still working their way to heaven. You shouldn't put too much stock in it for yourself. Anyway, if you really want it, God will know and see to it that you get your wish."

This was truly comforting, and I decided to take things in stride. I'd let God decide.

As we were entering Our Lady of Guadalupe Church on Sunday morning, Father Eugene Dubois was greeting his congregation at the door. "Good morning, Ray. Who's this lovely young lady you've brought to Mass today?"

"Father Eugene, I'd like you to meet my little sister, Iris. She'll be staying with me for a while," Ray said.

"Welcome, Iris. Where are you from?" Father Eugene's question was innocent enough, but we hadn't discussed much about my prior life.

"I'm from Florida," I answered, not adding any more. I glanced at Ray and saw that he was satisfied with my answer.

"Florida. Warm country over there, eh?" Father Eugene continued with the small talk.

I said, "I like winter because it's not so hot, but Florida is warmer than here right now."

"Father Eugene, Iris would like to join the church. Since she went to Catholic schools all her life, I wonder if she could join the RCIA class now and be baptized at the Easter Vigil along with the present group."

"If you went to Catholic schools all your life, Iris, why didn't you receive the sacraments as a child?"

"I was never baptized," I explained. "My parents wanted me to make the choice for myself later. They didn't practice any religion."

"But, Ray, I thought you told me your parents were devout—"

"Iris is much younger than I am, Father. She was raised differently," Ray interjected. "Our parents are now both active in the church."

Father said, "Just go into church now. We can discuss this after Mass."

Ray tugged at my elbow and guided me into the church before Father Eugene could ask any more questions.

"See you later, Father," I called over my shoulder. No harm in being friendly.

"Till after Mass." Father Eugene reached out his hand to greet the next group of people approaching him.

"Whoa! That was a lot more complicated than I thought it would be." Ray was perspiring. "Did we do any lying?"

"I don't think so," I whispered as we entered the church.

Lying. That brought back memories. I was pretty good at not lying back in high school. I was the queen of skirting the truth.

"Iris, what time did you come in last night?"

"I'm not sure. I didn't look at the clock." I had looked at it after a while, but not at the exact moment when I came in.

"Was it after eleven?"

"I'm pretty sure it was. I'm sorry. We got stuck in traffic."

Actually, we had left late, but you can almost always depend on Honolulu traffic to hold you up.

"Traffic? At eleven o'clock at night?"

"There was an accident."

The subject was successfully changed. They wanted to know how serious it was and whether anyone seemed to be hurt.

"Well, you should take the possibilities of delay into account and make sure you're not late. And let me remind you one more time never to ride with anyone who's been drinking or doing drugs. It's a dangerous world out there, and a driver needs her wits about her."

They knew I wouldn't do anything stupid or bad, so they didn't seem to worry much about how late I came in. It made me wonder about how much they loved me. I guess they just trusted me.

I whispered, "Ray, it depends on how you define a lie. In the strictest sense, I think we told one because we let him believe that we shared the same set of parents. Maybe we should just be cousins."

"I'm afraid the damage is done now." Ray thought for a moment. "I'll call Carol about it when we get home," he said.

I wanted to ask him who Carol was, but the Mass was starting. The entrance hymn was "You Are Near." I didn't know it, but my concentrated study of music helped me follow along nicely. The lyrics seemed appropriate:

Yahweh, I know you are near,
Standing always at my side.
You guard me from the foe,
And you lead me in ways everlasting.

The words calmed me down. As I sang, I felt peace returning to me. I felt like everything would turn out all right—even though we had possibly messed up badly. When it was time to pray for the needs of the people, I added a silent prayer. "Lord, I know you're watching. You said, 'Ask and you shall receive,' so I'm asking. Please help us out of this predicament. It means a lot to Ray. Thank you." It was my first real prayer, and I felt good about it.

After Mass, we tried to sneak away, but Father Eugene stopped us. He asked us to stop by the rectory during the week to discuss my matter. In the meantime, I could join the RCIA class in session and see how I felt about the material being presented. They met on Monday evenings at six and usually made it a brown bag supper. That week was a potluck. I didn't have to bring anything, but if I wanted to, I could. Ray should also come as my sponsor.

We thanked Father Eugene and walked away quickly, hoping to revamp our plans. I said a quick thank you to God as we walked. I had the feeling that everything would work out.

"Yes, it was a mistake to introduce her as your sister," Carol said later that morning. "But I can understand your thought processes. We'll have to ask for a change. God doesn't like to get involved, but this time—and since it's only one person—he may be willing to help."

As soon as Ray had called Carol with our problem, she had come over to his apartment. I could tell right away that she was a spirit. She was a strikingly beautiful woman with shoulder-length blonde hair and blue eyes, about my height, and with a nice figure to boot. But what hit me was the sense of peace written all over her face. It was just like the expressions on the faces of the saints in Old Bethlehem.

"Iris, this is my boss, Carol," Ray said.

"Hi, Iris. It's nice to meet you. I've heard so much about you. I hope you'll be able to help us," Carol said as she sat down in the living room. "Now, Ray, tell me again about your problem."

Ray told her the story of what had happened, and Carol came up with the astonishing thought that God could change things for us. The new plan would be that I was Ray's cousin. Everything else would remain the same. The only person God would have to interfere with would be Father Eugene. We would get down on our knees, right then and there, explain to God what had happened, and ask that he make the necessary change.

Carol and Ray made the sign of the cross. I followed suit. We began, "Our Father, Who art in heaven…"

I thought about the "Our Father" part.

"You said that we're all sisters and brothers under your mantle. Everyone on earth shares you as our heavenly Father. A father provides for his children's needs, protects them against danger, counsels, and guides them. Why are there so many starving and suffering people on earth? If you are the Father, the Provider, and you're all-powerful, why aren't they better provided for?"

"Iris, we did not bring misery into the world. Since man has free will—and we have no intention of taking that away—we will not help anyone who does not ask for it. And we will not interfere with what is happening in the world itself. We are always willing to give people the courage to face their troubles on earth, so that they can find eternal happiness with us in heaven. Remember that man's time on earth is nothing compared to eternity."

The Lord had spoken to me in my heart, and I found that I understood things better than I ever had before. Ray and Carol were busy petitioning God to help with the current dilemma, but I was making my own strides deep inside my heart. I joined in the petition, but I couldn't put much emotion into it. It seemed that in the grand scheme of things, this was a minor glitch. If God chose not to make a change in Father Eugene's memory, I would return to heaven. Melody would be—or would not be—helped, but the final result, for God's purposes, would be approximately the same. On the other hand, if he did intervene, that meant he had a special plan that was hinging on this project. I decided to wait and see. Whatever happened, I would do his will.

"Okay," Carol said. "Now we wait and see what happens when you see Father Eugene."

CHAPTER 15

Melody

Monday was a long day—my first day of going to work with Ray. We went to eight o'clock Mass. Ray went to Mass every day, and I thought that might be a good idea for me as well. I was nervous about my first heavenly assignment and prayed a short prayer as we walked. *Lord, please let me know how to act today in order to help Melody in the best way possible.*

Father Eugene was greeting everyone as they left Mass. Ray and I gave each other a nervous look as I grabbed my guitar at the door, but we really had no need to worry.

"Who's this lovely young lady you've brought along to Mass, Ray?" he asked.

"Father, this is my cousin, Iris. Iris, this is Father Eugene Dubois." Ray tried to act nonchalant, but he had to work at hiding his relief.

"It's good to meet you, Father." I extended my hand to him.

"Iris would like to join the RCIA class and become a member of the church, Father." Ray's confidence had returned.

"She went to Catholic schools as a child, but her parents wanted it to be her choice when she joined the church, so now she's ready."

"Did you have religion classes in your Catholic schools, Iris?" Father Eugene asked.

"Yes, Father. Every day. It was required of all students. I think I know most of the basics, and I could study to catch up."

"Come to the class tonight at six. Bring a sack lunch or, better yet, something to share. We're having a potluck supper tonight. You can try a few sessions and see how you feel about it, okay?"

Father Eugene was much more informal than I had expected. The priests I remembered from my childhood, although friendly, had been much more formal. Father Eugene's casual air helped me feel more comfortable with the whole unusual situation. Maybe I would make my First Communion, after all.

We stopped at a restaurant for breakfast. Ray had bacon, eggs, grits, and toast. I wanted a bagel with cream cheese and jam, but I had to settle for a biscuit with butter and jam. The biscuit was fresh and homemade, so I enjoyed it just as well. Ray promised we'd go to a deli the next morning.

It was just a twenty-minute walk from the restaurant to the center where Ray and Carol worked. I spent the day there, meeting the young people who frequented it and talking to them and the staff. The guitar piqued their interest, and a lot of them asked me to play their favorite songs for them. I didn't know all of them, and it was clear that the influence of heaven wasn't helping me with the ones I knew, but it was still a handy ice-breaker. Over lunch, Ray told his coworkers I was his cousin from Florida, and I was going to stay with him for a while.

In the afternoon, more people came in to play basketball, volleyball, or billiards. I joined in the fun as if I were just another neighborhood kid. It was exhilarating to run and jump with other people my own age who were there to let off a little steam. After a while, Melody appeared. She stood on the edge of the volleyball court with crossed arms and a tough look. She was obviously pretending that being included was the farthest thing from her mind.

I stole a glance in her direction every now and then and wondered what to do. In the old days, before I died, I would've made an immediate attempt to include the girl in the activity. I could always instinctively tell what a person needed, but I had also been overanxious to help. It took me a long time to learn that being too friendly was grounds for suspicion.

Lord, please help me know what to do to help her. I don't want to blow it on my very first day. Right away, I felt the Lord's presence fill my heart. I relaxed and decided to let things happen.

I had never been much of an athlete on earth, and I knew that I was surely not going to impress Melody with my prowess as a volleyball player. I had to really concentrate on relaxing and letting things happen. It was my serve, and I reminded myself that the game was just for fun. I did my best, but the ball hit the net anyway. What's new?

One of my teammates said, "Iris, let Melody take your place. She really knows how to play!"

The Lord had chosen his way to get Melody in, and I left the court in shame. Melody took my place, her eyes haughty with pride. She surely wouldn't be interested in getting to know me now. I wondered if God knew what he was doing.

"Hey! That's not fair!" someone from the other team shouted. "You can't have Melody on your team. You have to finish with the one you started with."

Apparently, winning was a high priority in this place.

Right away, a staff member became involved.

"Okay, what's up?" he asked with a tone of authority. "Melody?"

"The new girl was tired, and they asked me to take over," she said.

"Really, Iris? You were tired?"

I didn't want to lie. I wasn't tired. I'm never tired. But I didn't want to lose face with Melody.

"I really would like a breather, Josh. I must be out of shape," I said. An almost lie, just like in high school.

Josh didn't push the issue. "After you catch your wind, get back in and let Melody out. We usually start and end all games with the same players. Melody can play the next game."

"Okay." I decided I'd return in seven minutes. I looked at the clock; it was 3:22. At exactly 3:29, I'd get back in. By then, my turn to serve would be over for sure.

At exactly 3:29, I got up and went to where Melody was standing on the court, touched her on the arm, smiled, and thanked her for helping out. Melody looked at me coolly and returned to the sidelines. I couldn't really expect her to be friendly in that situation. I'd just try not to get involved in her sports. Or maybe I could ask her for a few pointers…

After that game, I wasn't picked for the next one. Melody was picked first, and I stayed to see what was so special about her. It didn't take long to figure out that she was a natural. She had strong arms and was well coordinated. She was taller than me—about five foot ten—and used her body well on the court. We obviously didn't have sports in common.

I got up to get a Coke from the machine. It was only fifty cents. What a deal! I wondered who sponsored this center. Obviously, they weren't out to make a profit. The place was clean, bright, airy, and cheerful. It didn't cost anything to use it. The snacks and drinks were downright cheap. Ray was obviously making enough money at it, and it wasn't understaffed either. I would have to ask Ray about it.

As I sat down to watch the game, Carol came and asked if she could sit with me.

"Of course." I took my guitar off the chair beside me.

"Are you enjoying yourself, Iris?" Carol asked as she sat down.

"Ya. This is great! I was just wondering who sponsors this place. It's really cool."

"It's paid for by a group of civic-minded citizens who realize that inner-city kids need a place to meet and be themselves. It's not subsidized by any government, local or federal, so we don't have to deal with budget cuts. That's a blessing, you know."

"Oh, I sure do," I said. "I used to go to a center for the mentally ill that was subsidized by the government. When I started, there were morning and afternoon activities, like group counseling, crafts, and band. And lunch was served every day. When they finished with the budget cuts, we were reduced to just the meal at lunchtime and no groups or other activities at all. You can imagine what that meant to all those people who had nothing else to do all day. It seems like they always cut in the wrong places. Anyway, I guess not many people care about the mentally ill."

"Or the poor," Carol added. "At least we have some good benefactors here, and we're trying to make the most of this situation. You know, there are some mental health issues here too, Iris. Maybe you could give us a few pointers."

"Maybe," I answered hesitantly. I was no mental health expert. I couldn't imagine what kind of advice I could give.

Ray joined us, and Carol excused herself to do some paperwork.

"I saw you playing volleyball," Ray said.

"Oh, brother. I guess everyone around knows I can't play now."

I wasn't really hurt, but it wasn't an uplifting thought just the same.

"Hey, you're not here to shine as an athlete, you know."

"Oh, I know," I said, smiling.

Just then, the group that had been playing volleyball came into the snack area for drinks and a rest. Melody sneaked a glance at me out of the corner of her eye, but her face was a sneer, so I made no attempt to communicate with her. It wasn't going to be easy. It was all I could do to be patient and bide my time. It felt like the depression was trying to take over again.

The group of volleyball players was laughing and joking at the two tables they had noisily pulled together near the Coke machine. My first thought was that they were laughing at me. They weren't. I told myself it was just the depression. I also told myself it was nice that Melody had friends to be with and talk to. *My* feelings didn't really count. I thanked God for helping me keep my thoughts straight.

"Iris, I have to stay here a bit longer, but you can go over to the apartment and make the food for your potluck tonight if you want."

Ray was finished with his break, had gathered his stack of papers, and was reaching into his jeans pocket for his keys. He was poised for a quick move away from the table. I took the keys and smiled at him, but I wasn't sure I'd leave just yet.

"I'll stop by your office and let you know when I'm leaving," I said.

As I thought about what I wanted to make for the potluck, I absent-mindedly stared at the volleyball players. I watched their body language and listened to their conversation. As I did that, I understood something about the dynamics of the group. They were all unsure of themselves, despite boisterous shows of self-confidence. Of course, they probably all came from pretty difficult circumstances. Even those who had stable home lives lived with the problems of poverty in modern-day America. They had felt the pain of discrimination in their school situations, probably had never been expected to rise above their circumstances, and so on.

"They would benefit from some of our love," the Lord's familiar voice said in my heart.

I agreed.

"Hey, Iris," someone in the volleyball group said. "Come on over and sit with us!"

It seemed like a kind gesture that I hadn't expected, but when I got there, I found out why I had been invited.

"Melody wants to know if you're Ray's girlfriend. She has a major crush on him," one of the guys said before I even sat down. I had noticed the same guy before, mooning over Melody.

"Ray?" I said in surprise. "He's, like, thirty-five years old!" Oops! I hoped I hadn't given something away because Ray didn't look that old. "Anyway, he's my cousin. I don't have any dibs on him."

I looked at Melody and noticed she was blushing. Now that was interesting. I'd have to bring this up with Ray. No, on second thought, I decided to wait and see what developed.

"Well, gotta go now," I announced to the ensuing silence. "See ya tomorrow."

"Bye," most of the group said. I noticed that Melody was looking down at the table and ignoring me.

CHAPTER 16

A Romance Novel

I had no trouble finding my way back to Ray's apartment. On the way, I spoke to no one and occupied my mind with deciding what I wanted to cook. Since Ray didn't have the usual ingredients for black bean soup, bean dip, or nachos, I decided to make hot dog hash. Mémère had invented it, and it was always a hit at potlucks. If you had hot dogs, potatoes, and an onion in the house, you could easily make it.

As I fried the onion in butter, I thought about Melody and her crush on Ray. Maybe she just liked him because he seemed to care about her. Maybe he was a safe person to like—from afar, so the other guys wouldn't hassle her with dating and so on. That was how I felt during my depression days. I didn't want the hassle of dating then either.

I added the chopped hot dogs, potatoes, and water, set the pot to simmer, and started reminiscing. At first, I was sure I was gay. I could feel true love for my good girlfriends. But then I met a guy I really cared about too. I thought I must be bisexual. Then the depression got so bad that I didn't want to think about what I was—or what I wanted. I didn't want to think about anything at all. I'm sure I just stumbled onto the whole "music in medicine" thing. I could do my music, which I loved, and do something good for people at the same time. (I really needed to do something good for people—all my life. It was a deep-down part of me.)

Reminiscing made the tears start rolling down my cheeks. I couldn't cry or laugh back when I was depressed. Just having the tears come out right now made everything better. I couldn't even remember the overwhelming feelings of despair I used to have. I wondered how things would've turned out if I hadn't died.

"You were on the right track, Iris. You would've found your way over time, but trust us, the shortcut is better."

I liked hearing the Lord's voice in my heart. I understood that because he was all-knowing, I could trust whatever he told me. This time, I thanked him for the shortcut. Life on earth had been getting pretty overwhelming.

When Ray came in the door, I had stopped crying and was smiling.

"I guess that depression has pretty much gone away, hasn't it?" he said cheerfully. Then he sniffed the air. "Yum! Smells good!"

"That's for the potluck," I told him in a bossy voice. "You'll just have to wait. You can have some crackers and peanut butter if you want."

Ray pretended to be downcast. "Oh, boy," he said.

We wanted to arrive a little early to get settled before class, so we left the apartment at five-thirty. Ray carried the hot dog hash in his nicest pot, and I carried the serving spoon. The parish hall had a small kitchen with a stove, and the oven was warm. The instructor, David Desrosiers, introduced himself and showed me the book and where they were up to while Ray put the hot dog hash in the oven. David told me I would receive a Bible of my own at Mass on the following Sunday—my first Bible.

As I sat through my first RCIA class, I noticed that the people seeking entry into the Catholic church were no different than anybody else, except that they were intent on establishing a lifelong relationship with God. They weren't perfect. They openly admitted some of their faults, but they all agreed that God understood their weaknesses. They believed they needed his love and guidance in every aspect of their lives, and they were confident that God would stay with them as long as they trusted in him. It was a special blessing that I wished I had had in my lifetime. On the other hand, I might not have even noticed if God had reached out to me back then.

"We tried," Jesus said. I was sure it was true. I just hadn't been in a position to listen.

On the way home, I was tempted to tell Ray about Melody's crush on him, but something inside me told me to keep it to myself. It was only a crush and wasn't likely to become a problem for some time. Instead, I commented on the stars in the sky.

When we reached his apartment, I was happy but exhausted. I believed that my stay on earth was going to be a productive learning experience. I was optimistic that all would go better than Ray or I had ever hoped. It was nice to feel so optimistic, and I didn't allow any doubts to enter my thoughts and spoil the good feeling. I slept like a baby that night and awoke refreshed and optimistic about the day to come.

At Mass, I listened carefully to the day's readings and did my best to understand what they were about. The gospel was about sick people hoping to just touch Jesus's robes and be healed. And it happened because they had faith! I decided I needed to have that kind of faith in God. If I calmly trusted him, everything would go according to his plan. There was no need to worry or try to change things. It was a nice thought and a good feeling, but I wondered if I could do it.

True to his word, Ray took me to a deli for bagels. I chose an everything bagel slathered with a thick layer of cream cheese and a piece of lox on top. Ray had the same on a plain bagel.

"Garlic and onions in the morning?" he exclaimed. "Are you afraid of vampires or something? Remind me to stay away from you today." He smiled. "You seem happy today."

"Yup. I guess the depression's gone," I answered cheerfully and took a big bite of my bagel, washing it down with Earl Grey tea.

As we ate, we talked a little about the kids I had met and how they were impressed by the guitar. Then we went to the center. Ray went about his business, and I roamed around from group to group, still getting acquainted, still trying to play their favorite songs. Word spreads quickly in a small community, and everyone soon knew that I was Ray's cousin and not his girlfriend. They mostly liked Ray, so they accepted me too. In no time, I fit right in.

However, my depression was not as gone as I would have liked to think. There were still days when I felt left out because of something someone said. But I was able to talk myself out of the hopeless feelings. The good days were gaining on the bad ones, so I had every reason to feel positive about the whole situation.

About two weeks after I arrived, Melody finally approached me. We had seen each other nearly every day, but we hadn't spoken. I found it hard to stay away from her, but I knew it was what I needed to do. I had to wait patiently for Melody to make the first move.

"Did you tell Ray that I was in love with him?" she asked in a tone that was a little too belligerent.

"No," I replied. I felt some confusion, but it was a relief that I could answer her truthfully.

"Then how do you explain that he's treating me nicer?" Melody said.

I thought for a moment before answering.

"Maybe he likes you, too," I said with a shrug. I realized it could be a problem for Ray if I set him up as liking Melody, but it was Melody who had noticed the change. I could only reply as if I didn't know anything about the situation. Besides, it was obvious that Ray liked the kid.

"Do you think he does?" Melody asked with anticipation in her voice. Her expression showed it too.

I had to be careful. I spoke in an unemotional tone, trying to appear detached about the whole subject.

"He hasn't said anything to me, and I really don't know why he's nicer to you than he used to be. Honest! I didn't mention anything to him. I don't think that's any of my business."

I thought I had acted that pretty well. I hoped she thought I really didn't care. I started to collect my trash and leave the little table where I had been eating lunch, but Melody sat down across from me and said, "I know about you, you know."

I was taken aback. What did she know? Could she have figured out that I was a spirit? How? Did she know about Ray and Carol too? Deep down, the Lord was telling me not to worry, but I wanted so much to succeed in this mission that it was hard not to.

"I saw you in the Salvation Army," Melody said.

My relief was almost as great as my shame in not trusting the Lord. I had forgotten about the incident in the dressing room. What would be a believable reaction? I asked the Lord for help. I opened my mouth to speak.

"So? What difference does that make?"

The tone was not a part of me. I wasn't acting; my mouth was doing the talking on its own.

"I could tell Ray."

That was a useful thought. I let the Lord go on with this conversation.

"So? What makes you think he cares?"

"Are you serious? We all watched him when you first came, and we all thought you were the one he was gonna marry. I mean, the guy was all over you with his eyes! I know he cares, and I know he'll be really mad when he finds out."

Melody seemed inappropriately vindictive, and I wondered what she was looking for. Again, I deferred to the Lord.

"You're not gonna tell him, are you?"

There was a nervous anxiety in my voice. The Spirit was still guiding me along, and I didn't know where he was leading. It was really weird to let him take over, but I was glad just the same.

Melody looked pleased with herself. She seemed to think she had me right where she wanted me. Little did she know that God was in charge.

"I won't tell him if you do what I say," she answered.

Bribery? This is almost like a romance novel. I wonder what will happen next.

"What do you want?" I asked. This was really strange. I was glad I could trust God.

"Simple. I just want you to get us two together." Melody got up, turned, and walked away with a smug look.

I could've figured that out all by myself. But it just couldn't work! I should have told Ray all about it right away. On the other hand, I kind of liked the idea of the challenge. I wanted to wait a while and think about it some more. I blocked out the eerie feeling creeping up in the back of my mind.

That evening, at supper, I told Ray that Melody had approached me.

"Really? Did she confide in you?" He seemed thrilled. I wondered again how much he really liked her.

"You could say that," I answered. "She made me a proposition. In fact, she tried to bribe me." I was torn between telling him the whole story and not telling him.

"I'm all ears," Ray said.

"It's simple. She won't tell you about my self-mutilation if I do something for her."

No. I wasn't going to tell him. It was too exciting. That small voice inside me (could it be God?) was urging me to tell him the truth, but I ignored it. I wanted to see if I could work it out on my own.

"What do you have to do?" Ray asked.

"I have to help her snare the man of her dreams."

There. I could see about my very own romance novel. I had written plenty of poetry in my life, and I had started lots of stories but never finished one. Maybe this would be my chance. That night, I fell asleep scheming how I was going to work out my little intrigue to everyone's satisfaction.

Ray and Melody were walking along Bourbon Street during Mardi Gras. They had enjoyed a wonderful day, walking arm in arm through the crowded streets, dodging raucous merrymakers who smelled of alcohol and sported beaded necklaces in gaudy colors while lumbering along the historic street. There was a spirit of excitement all around them. People on the balconies were throwing down strings of beads to passersby who would display just the slightest bit of indecency, jazz music blared out of pubs and restaurants, and everyone was in high spirits.

I was watching Ray and Melody and wondering what they were up to. Ray's expression and actions were hard to decipher, but Melody was obviously on cloud nine. For her, it was a romantic evening.

Ray stopped, turned to Melody, and looked her straight in the face: her twinkling brown eyes surrounded by brown curly eyelashes, her smallish straight nose, and her broad smile that enhanced her overall beauty.

"You're beautiful," Ray said quietly.

He had a serious expression. I could see the dilemma on his face. Ray was in love with Melody, and she was obviously in love with him, but they could never be together as lovers. He was probably wondering how to end it without hurting her.

Melody must have sensed his quandary and asked, "What's the matter?"

"It's complicated," Ray answered. He took a deep breath and slowly let it out. "I'm no good for you. I could never love you the way you want to be loved. I could never promise to spend my life with you."

The happiness on Melody's face melted away immediately. The beautiful face was gone, the familiar hard expression taking over.

"Are you already married?" There was an edge to her voice, and tears were glistening in her eyes.

"It's more complicated than that." He paused. "I'm not really in charge of myself. I mean, I'm free to make my own decisions and everything..." He stopped explaining and answered her question. "I'm not married. But I *am* tied to another commitment that I can't explain."

"Did you make some kind of vow or something?"

She's gonna run! We might lose her. There's no telling what she'll do. She won't be able to face her shame at having been so foolishly in love with someone who didn't love her.

Ray opened his mouth to answer, but before anything came out, I rushed over and cried out, "No!"

Melody's reaction was instant. She turned and ran into the crowd. I flew over the people, looking for her. I saw her standing in the crowd, watching one of the many parades. Melody was poised to throw herself in front of a float.

Again, I screamed, "No!"

Ray was beside me. He said, "Wake up, Iris. You're having a bad dream." His voice was desperate.

Slowly, the parade, Bourbon Street, and the merrymakers disappeared from my view. The noise faded. I had been dreaming.

Ray was sitting on the edge of my bed and looking very concerned. He probably wasn't used to people having nightmares in his apartment.

"Thank you for waking me up. That was a pretty bad nightmare," I said quietly.

"Do you want to talk about it?" Ray asked.

He looked really worried. I wanted to tell him everything right away, but I didn't know where to start. I needed to digest it a little before we talked.

"Don't worry. It's not the depression," I said. "I have to think about the dream for a while, and then we can talk. Can I tell you about it tomorrow?"

"Okay, if that's what you want." Ray was visibly relieved, and he went back to his couch.

Poor guy. That must've been a real trip for him. I wondered if he was sorry he invited me to come.

That had been some dream. The Lord had taught me a lot with it. First of all, I didn't know I cared about Melody's feelings that much. And then, it made me wonder how Ray really felt about Melody. I mean, he did ask me to come help her. Maybe he was in love with her. I knew now that the Lord wanted me to tell Ray that Melody loved him. It wasn't a game. It was real life, and Melody could be seriously hurt. Her love for Ray was real. It wasn't fair of me to play with it. That could make her feel unlovable, just like I felt when I was her age. I wouldn't wish that on anybody.

I thanked the Lord for showing me where I was going wrong. I said, "You're my best friend!"

The next morning, I asked Ray whether he had any feelings for Melody.

"It's complicated, Iris," he started. "You know that carnal feelings are just that: carnal. I don't have carnal feelings for Melody, but in my heart, she's very special. I think I could have loved her if I had met her when I was alive. I don't know what attracts me to her, it must be that kind of chemistry that kindred spirits have. You and I are also kindred spirits, Iris, but it's different with Melody. I want to take her in my arms and take care of her, bring her happiness, and protect her. Do you understand?"

Yes, I understood. He was in love with Melody. Maybe not in the sexual sense, but truly in love. It wasn't just an attraction. It was a caring, nurturing love. But he was a spirit, and like he said in my dream, he couldn't meet her needs. Melody would never understand it.

"Well, you're the man of her dreams," I stated bluntly. I couldn't beat around the bush; I needed to make the problem clear. "And we have to do something about that before it becomes a problem that can't be solved."

CHAPTER 17

A Coping Strategy

Ray looked shocked at first, but as the thought became reality in his mind, a look of understanding took over.

"She does seem to drop by my office pretty often with unimportant questions or remarks." He paused. "But I never thought she was attracted to me."

"Think about it, Ray. She's a lonely girl. Probably feels totally unloved. Doesn't trust her peers. And this good-looking, steady-Eddie type of guy shows genuine interest in her. Of course, her heart is going to go pitter-patter."

"You're right. But I never intentionally—"

"Of course you didn't. And I'm not accusing you of it. But we do have a problem now, and we have to do something to solve it."

Ray took on a decisive tone. "First thing is prayer. Get your jacket. It's time for Mass. Let's walk in silence and listen for God's guidance."

Our footsteps echoed as we walked hand in hand through the empty streets. We were both silent, both wondering what to do about Melody, and both praying for guidance. I didn't know what was going through Ray's mind, but I prayed:

Lord, they say you work in mysterious ways. Did you have something to do with this attraction between Ray and Melody? If you did, do you have a plan for them? Please let me know what I can do to help fulfill your plan. It's pretty scary to think that we might lead her to suicide, which can't possibly be your holy will. Please don't put that kind of responsibility on my shoulders. Just help me to make things good for Melody. Please.

Father Eugene was at the entrance to the church, and he greeted us with a friendly smile.

"What have we here, kissing cousins?" he joked, pointing to our hands still held together.

"Oh no, Father." Ray immediately released my hand. He quickly regained his composure and added, "Just kindred spirits communicating."

I had to smile.

Over breakfast at the deli, we tried to put together a plan of action. Neither of us was able to come up with something that we believed would work.

"I have to get across to her that I don't love her in that way, and when I do, she may want to die— literally. And if we try to steer her toward another man, she's likely to figure it out and have the same reaction."

"What if we just wait—and hope and pray— that she does get interested in another man."

"She'll have to be less interested in me first," Ray said. "I don't want to start being mean to her—"

"No, no, no. Just act naturally," I said. "But keep your distance—and be sure not to let on that I told you anything!"

I was afraid of what she might do to me if she found out. I had never actually been in a fistfight.

I thought for a minute and came up with an idea. "I know what. I'll put on a friendlier act so she gets the feeling that I care. Maybe I can become a confidante. That could buy us some time. A good friend is sometimes better than a boyfriend."

"Well, that'll be a start, I guess, but I'm afraid she isn't going to give up easily. Being friendly but distant will be a problem for me, but it's the only good thought we've come up with so far. I'll talk to Carol about it too. Maybe she'll have an idea. Let's go to work."

Ray seemed worried as we walked toward the center. I reminded myself to fully rely on God and said a silent prayer. I was determined to find a way to befriend Melody. Maybe I could ask her for some pointers on volleyball, like, how to serve.

Melody didn't come to the center that day or the next or for the rest of the week. In a way, it was good because it gave us time to think things out more, but it was also a problem. She had never stayed away so long before. We didn't know what to do about this new development.

Finally, Carol had an idea. "Iris, the center has a policy of not allowing employees to search out clients in their homes, but you're not an employee. You could just go look her up, on some pretense, and find out what her problem is."

"She'll be suspicious. We aren't exactly friends, you know."

"That's true, but you could have news about Ray, and you could've snuck into his file and gotten her address."

I considered this a few minutes. "Okay. I'll give it a try, but we'll have to work out what the news is about Ray. And what if I found out some deep, dark secret about her while looking up her address in the file?"

"There are no secrets in her file," Ray said. "We don't keep that kind of information on file. But let's wait until Monday to see if she shows up. That'll give us time to prepare a plan of attack, so to speak. Iris, maybe you can ask some of the kids if they know anything about her."

The three of us agreed on Ray's and Carol's idea and got back to our routines. Carol had a meeting with the board of directors, Ray was giving a class on job responsibility, and I played. My job was playing, and I took it seriously. I had forced myself to play volleyball—even though I wasn't any good at it—because I saw it as my job. And lo and behold, I was getting better. I was still the worst player around, but I could see some improvement. Even some of the guys told me I was learning. I could almost feel the daggers coming from the girls whenever one of the boys complimented me, but I had to accept it as a fact of life for this particular group of young adults.

Most of them probably don't have a clue about what self-esteem is—never mind possessing any of it. It's no wonder they see me as a threat to their relationships with the men of the group. No, not men. They're just big boys looking for sex.

I had the feeling the Holy Spirit wasn't happy with my thoughts, but I continued uninterrupted.

It would be so nice to introduce these girls to more stable and mature men. Then they might have a chance for a meaningful life of togetherness. On the other hand, I wonder how many mature men might take advantage of vulnerable girls from questionable circumstances.

These kinds of thoughts always appealed to the depressive side of my personality, and I could sense the Holy Spirit trying to pull me away from them. He was encouraging me—no, pushing me—to find a meaningful distraction. I was enjoying myself, deriving a certain sadistic pleasure in feeling down, but the Holy Spirit refused to allow it. I felt forced into making a new sort of decision. I had to find something constructive to do that would raise my spirits. I got up from my regular table in the gym, picked up my guitar, and turned toward the classrooms while struggling with my mind and my attitude. I reached the art studio and considered going in to draw a picture that depicted how I felt, but the Spirit stopped me dead in my tracks.

"No more feeling sorry for yourself, Iris. You've portrayed your feelings in pictures and writing enough times. Try something new. Drop the sad feelings, and find a distraction that will do good for someone else."

The Lord was right. I never did control my depression through art or any other activities. I would try his way. I'd get involved in some positive activity. As I turned around to go back to where the crowd was, I glanced into the window of the art studio. Hal, a man with Down's syndrome, had been hired by the center to do light janitorial work. He was looking at all the colors of paint in the tubes, his broom leaning against his side. He seemed to be trying to sound out the names of the colors.

I opened the door. As I walked in, Hal looked up. His broom fell to the floor. He wasn't afraid of being found not doing his work. The center paid him for the work he did—not the work he was supposed to do—but Hal didn't know me well. He probably wasn't sure how I would treat him.

I was nervous about Hal. I had no concept about the mentally challenged. I was leery because I remembered the mentally ill people I had lived with in a group home, people who would never advance beyond that particular level of group home. Some had been schizophrenics who conversed with angels or demons. Much as I wanted to care about them, I had still been afraid to get too close to them. But Hal wasn't like that. Mentally challenged is different. Hal was quiet and gentle.

I said, "Hi, Hal."

"I want to paint a picture of a flower for my mom, but I can't find yellow. She likes yellow roses. I know *yellow* starts with *y*, but I can't find any color that starts with *y*," he said.

"Do you want me to help you?" I asked.

"Yeah. I found this one that starts with *sun*. That might be yellow." In his hand, he held a tube of paint.

I slowly walked over to where he stood. "Sunburst," I read. "Yup, that's a good one." I smiled and started to relax in the presence of this man, who was pretty much a stranger to me.

Hal took the paint to the long worktable where he had already laid a sheet of green construction paper, pulled up a folding chair, and started to open the tube of sunburst paint. He bit on his tongue as he concentrated on the screw top. Grandpa used to do that. (Smile. Happy memory.) He carefully squirted a dab of paint out on a palette, which he had forgotten to bring closer to him from the center of the table.

After screwing the top back on the tube, he slid the palette closer to his workspace and reached across the bright yellow dollop to get a brush from the collection of supplies. Some of the paint got on the sleeve of his flannel shirt.

"Oh no!" he exclaimed as he rubbed at the spot. "This is a new shirt! Mom's gonna kill me!" The rubbing made the spot even larger and more noticeable.

I soaked the corner of a paper towel in paint remover and approached him. "Here. This will take some of it off. It won't show so much."

When I reached over to rub the stain, Hal suddenly pulled away.

"Don't touch me!" he yelled. "What is that?"

I was surprised by his tone. I took a deep breath and swallowed. "It's just something to remove some of the paint so it doesn't look so bad." I couldn't completely hide my frustration and anger.

Hal was ashamed. "Sorry I yelled at you. I lose control sometimes. Give it to me, and I'll try. I don't even know your name." He clumsily worked at the sleeve and got paint all over the paper towel and his hands.

"Maybe if you stand up, away from your work, and take your shirt off…"

Hal was mollified by my words. He rose clumsily from his chair, letting it fall with a clang, and moved to a clear end of the table.

"Could you please help me take it off?" he asked. "I have paint all over my hands."

I did my best to help remove his shirt and put it on the table. "Do you want me to try to clean it with another paper towel?" I asked.

I had to remember that Hal was a man and not a kid. I had to give him a chance to decide how he wanted to proceed.

He tried to wipe the paint off his hands "You can try, but I still don't know your name."

That detail was obviously important to him.

"Sorry. My name is Iris. I'm Ray's cousin." I dipped another paper towel in the paint remover and rubbed off most of the paint. "See? If you start on the outside and work your way in, it doesn't spread—and you can get most of it off." I looked up and held it up for him to see. "I've had a lot of practice. I get it all over myself when I'm painting." I stretched it across a chair to dry. "It should be pretty dry when you're ready to go home."

"Thank you, Iris. That looks pretty good. Do you know how to paint too?" Hal picked up the folding chair and opened it in front of his workspace.

"I know a little about painting," I answered. "What do you want to know?"

"I want to paint my mom a rose, but I'm not sure how to do it. Do you know how to paint a rose?"

I thought about it. My sister Claire had learned to draw a rose in fifth grade. She had shown me how to make a simple center and add petals all around until it looks like a rose. Pretty easy. Almost anyone could do it. With paint, it might be a problem. Olivia's process was also simple when she painted her Bauernstil flowers. I felt confident that I could help Hal. The Holy Spirit was sending me these memories just in time. I thanked him in my heart. It was nice to think of happy times with my sisters.

"Here's something I learned from one of my sisters," I said as I drew a simple rose in pencil on scrap paper. "I can help you draw this on your paper and you can color it in with yellow paint. Or I can show you how to do one with just paint strokes."

"I like coloring it in. I'm real good at coloring," Hal said with a smile. "Can you teach me how to draw one on my paper, please, Iris?"

I used to think it was a pain to say please all the time. This time, it added a nice flair to the request, and I liked it. I taught

Hal the process of drawing a rose, and once he had caught on, he decided to draw three big ones across his paper. By then, the paint had dried on his palette, and he had to squeeze out more. He was good with the paintbrush, though, and when he finished, his three roses looked pretty good. At least, he was proud of them. I was also proud of them. I didn't know what he would have drawn or painted without my help, but I could see that he considered the flowers the best he could do.

"I'm gonna let this dry on the chair with my shirt," he said. "I'll pick it up before I go home for dinner. Mom's gonna love it!" He tidied up his work-space, picked up his broom, and said, "Thank you, Iris. God bless you!"

What could I say in response?

"God bless *you*!" I said. That made me really happy. I had completely forgotten the depression that had been building up earlier. I had found a true coping mechanism. From now on, I'll reach out beyond my own worries and help someone else.

"Thank you, Lord." I sat in Hal's chair, took a large sheet of sketch paper, and drew a scene of horses in a meadow with mountains in the background— maybe the Grand Tetons. The sun was setting (or rising) behind the mountains, and the horses were lazily grazing and swatting flies with their tails. Their young were frolicking, stretching and testing their muscles, and taunting each other to the chase. It was summer, and there were no worries. Although it was winter in New Orleans, I had no worries at that particular moment. I savored the peace.

CHAPTER 18

Melody's Problem

On Monday, Melody didn't show up at the center, and none of the center's regular clients had any information about her. She hadn't gone to school. Percy, the boy who had asked me if I was Ray's girlfriend, claimed not to know what was going on.

Carol, Ray, and I agreed that it was time for me to call on her at her home address. I would tell her that Ray was looking for work closer to home, in Florida. It might force Melody to try harder to snatch him, but it was the only good reason we could think of for me to go to her house.

Melody lived in a run-down housing project. I had seen projects like that in my lifetime, but I had never walked through one. My family had always avoided driving through those areas. There were lots of movies about the bad things that happened in housing projects. Some were about normal people accidentally landing in the middle of a dangerous area. You got the feeling the residents would enjoy harming them or even killing them.

I had never thought about what life would be like for the people who lived in a place like this. (Movies and TV weren't real, right?) Could Melody be used to it? I couldn't imagine how anyone could get used to it. You might learn not to go out at night, not to answer the door, or to be careful peeking out the windows. I wondered what it was like for her to walk to school every day. Could there be any joy in her life? Just seeing this place made me feel so lucky. I felt I had no right to complain about anything in my life.

I finally found the door to Melody's apartment: 4-D. The doorway needed a paint job, and it looked like someone had tried to damage the lock. (They probably had more than one lock on the inside.) I timidly knocked on the door. There was no answer. I knocked harder.

Melody opened the door a crack and peeked around it. I opened my mouth to say hi, but Melody slammed the door shut before I could utter a word.

"No, Melody." I knocked again and yelled, "I have to tell you something." I almost blurted out the news about Ray right there, but then I remembered the neighbors. Melody probably wouldn't want them to hear anything.

"Go away!" Melody yelled from inside. "And don't come back!"

Okay. I didn't expect her to invite me in for coffee. I yelled, "When will you be coming to the center? I really do have some news you'll be interested in."

There wasn't a sound from inside the apartment. Finally, Melody opened the door again and peeked out.

"Is it about Ray?" she asked. She was wearing pajamas and shivering a little in the cool air of the doorway.

"Are you sick?" I asked. She tried to shut the door again, but I had stuck my foot in the opening. I quickly delivered my message. "Ray is looking for work in Fort Lauderdale and Tampa. I thought you should know."

Melody said, "I'll come by the center tomorrow." She seemed calm, which surprised me. When she turned away, she mumbled, "Thanks for telling me."

And that was that. I was finished with my major task. I walked back to the center and reported to Ray. He wasn't satisfied. He fired questions at me. "Why was she in her pajamas? Did she look sick? Was she pale? Why hasn't she been coming here? What does her place look like?"

"Boy, Ray, you have it bad," I said, and he calmed down. I couldn't answer his questions. I did tell him that the area was pretty bad, but he already knew that. We would just have to wait until the next day for answers.

Melody returned to the center the next day. She was subdued. I was careful not to run up to her and greet her. All the kids offered nonchalant greetings: "Hey, kid. Where ya been?" and "Look out! She's back." It was clear that almost everyone was happy to see her. Ray had been in and out of his office all morning, but once she appeared, he kept his distance.

She dragged a chair to my table and plopped herself down.

"Are you okay? Were you sick?" I put down my guitar.

"You could say that." She turned to look at the volleyball game.

"Was it a flu or something?"

"None of your business. Where's Ray?"

Well, what could I expect? We weren't friends. But why was she sitting here and asking a question she already knew the answer to?

"He's probably in his office."

"He's not gone?"

It took a moment for me to realize she was asking about whether Ray had already left for Florida. "No, he's still looking for places closer to his parents."

Melody got up and went toward the offices. I pretended not to care and to be tuning my guitar. I wondered what Melody's problem was. Maybe she had had an abortion. There was probably another cherub flying around heaven right now. Well, that might be better than down here in the projects.

"Melody was pretty upset about me wanting to go to Florida," Ray said as we sat down to eat dinner that night. "I really had no idea she thought so much of me."

"Well, I've seen how concerned you are about her. She could easily have misinterpreted that for true love. She probably hasn't experienced much true love in her life. Were you able to convince her that you care about her but don't love her?"

"Did you think I could?" Ray was clearly frustrated. "She stormed out of the office and left the center before I could explain anything. I don't know what to do about it."

"Did she tell you why she hadn't been around?" "Abortion. She didn't want to run into the guy—one of our guys. He wanted to get married, but she didn't want to marry him. She says she won't raise kids in the projects. Having the abortion made her feel down, like there was no way out." Ray paused. "It's good she doesn't want to have kids while living in the projects, but why the abortion? Aren't there ways to avoid pregnancy so that they don't have to have an abortion? I got the feeling it wasn't her first one either. Maybe that's why it made her feel down. It makes me mad. I feel like I could explode. Just look at her life. Look at all their lives. There doesn't seem to be a way out for them. What kind of world is this?" He turned his eyes to heaven. "Why, God?"

I wondered why too. People were growing up in these conditions without having asked for any of it. And they continued to live that way and bring up children in it. It was a vicious cycle. Why? It didn't make sense. If it was some kind of freedom of choice, I didn't want any of it. I couldn't imagine anyone wanting any of it.

God whispered in my ear, "Sometimes, one person's freedom of choice infringes upon another's. You, Raymond, and Carol are there to show that we love all our children. They must learn to hope in us."

We're supposed to help people find hope in you? For what? How would that hope help them get out of a hopeless situation?

"Remember that earthly life is temporary. Your young cousins never gave up hope that they would someday get out of their wheelchairs. That didn't happen in their lifetimes, but in heaven, they're whole—for all eternity. You must help Melody find hope in our loving care and persevere during her lifetime to achieve something better for herself and for others."

I looked at Ray. "How do we give her hope?"

"Hope? You're kidding, right?" Ray rolled his eyes toward the ceiling.

Clearly not a good time to brainstorm. We cleared the table and washed the few dishes in silence. Then we said good night. Ray went to his couch, and I went to bed, both of us brooding over the situation with Melody.

God, she's eighteen years old, and she's had an abortion. I'm sure she doesn't want to be pitied, but I can't help feeling bad for her. She needs to be taken into a big hug by you. I can't imagine us being able to make her feel better. Please help her.

The next morning, things didn't look any better. It was a cold, gray day. We drank our coffee and went to church in silence. Breakfast didn't appeal to either of us. We just ordered toast and tea (Ray had coffee) and left without finishing. We walked to the center without sharing a single word.

When we arrived, I followed Ray into his office. I wanted my instructions for the day.

"I guess we're back to the confidante/friendship idea," Ray said. "Maybe we can help her figure this out that way."

I returned to my usual table in the gym. It was funny how I always sat in the same place. It was getting to be a habit. I watched a volleyball game as I strummed and let myself escape from the tension of the last twenty-four hours.

I had a great idea. There might be the possibility of a volleyball scholarship for Melody. That would be so cool. She could study whatever she wanted and be really popular as an athlete. I went to ask Ray about it.

"We've already tried that line," Ray said. "She wants to be a hairdresser and nothing else. Needless to say, there aren't any sports scholarships available for beauty school. And anyway, we may want to deal with the abortion first." He glanced at his computer screen. "I was just researching Rachel's Vineyard. Do you know what that is?"

"Never heard of it," I answered. "What is it?"

"I read about it in a parish bulletin a couple of months ago. They have weekend retreats for people who are recovering from abortions." Ray wrote down the phone number from the website. "They even have some for men. Anyway, I thought you could pretend to have had an abortion, and I could encourage Melody to go on a weekend with you. It might work."

Abortion? It hit me. I must have stuffed it in a deep, dark crevice of my brain. This was surely coming from God. That's the real reason for the shortcut!

Ray was staring at me.

What is my expression like?

"What?" he asked.

I looked at my cousin. Only God knew about this—and only because he knows everything.

In a very small voice, I said, "I wouldn't have to pretend."

Ray waited. I remember how much I appreciated that.

"I've never felt bad about it. I was on a lot of medications, tough stuff, and so was the guy. The baby wouldn't have been healthy, that's for sure. It was the best thing to do. At least, that's how I saw it then. I haven't thought about it since then. I bet it's one of the earthly things I have to deal with before I go on. I'll go on a weekend retreat with Melody—if she's willing. Are you thinking she might get some hope from it?"

"Let's look into it," Ray said. "You might even like it." He picked up the phone and started dialing. "I'll check when the next retreat is."

Lord, this is getting scary.

The comforting voice said, "Just trust us."

"Okay. April 7 to 9. That'll give us plenty of time to get ready," Ray said, covering the receiver with his hand. "Let's get you registered first. Then we can see about Melody."

I opened my mouth to protest.

"Don't worry," he said. "I'll cover that angle. Remember that I'm the man of her dreams. If I can't get her to do it, you can still opt out."

He anticipated the wrong question. Why should I have to go? I was already dead and in heaven. It wasn't going to do anything for me.

The Lord had his answer ready. "Iris, in order to continue to grow spiritually, you must confront your past. We gave you the shortcut because we knew you would never recover emotionally from the abortion. Your heart is too good. But now, with our help, you must face your sin and understand that you are loved unconditionally."

I would have a whole month to worry about the weekend. I was really going to need God's help.

Ray told Melody he loved her very much—but more like a daughter than a lover. He told her that he intended to remain celibate. (The Holy Spirit must have injected that idea into his head, and it was a good one.) Somehow, he got Melody to listen to him.

She agreed to go to the retreat weekend with me.

He helped her get registered, called the place whenever she had a question, and was able to show how much he cared without fear of leading her on.

In the evenings, he listened patiently to my misgivings and fears. He always found words of encouragement for me. I was even more strongly guided by the Lord, but I still found it hard to face the thought that I might have to confess this sin in front of others. The sleeplessness of my depression days started to haunt me a little. It wasn't as desperate as it had been back then. I usually slept well between one and six. Sometimes, I even fell asleep earlier.

At the center, I was preoccupied most of the time. I couldn't concentrate on what was going on. Everyone noticed. Some asked what was wrong, but I didn't tell them. Even Hal noticed something and asked if he could help. I smiled and thanked him, but I told him he couldn't help.

He said, "God bless you," before he turned away and continued sweeping.

"You too," I answered automatically.

On April 7, Ray borrowed the center's van and drove the two of us to the retreat house in Metairie. I took my overnighter out of the back and started toward the entrance.

Ray handed Melody her bag. "It's still up to you. I think you'll like it, but it has to be your decision," he said.

If Melody doesn't go in, neither will I.

"I'll go in," Melody said quietly. "Will you pick us up on Sunday?"

"Of course," Ray answered. He gave her a gentle hug.

CHAPTER 19

Healing Weekend

I had no idea what to expect from the weekend. My hands were shaking so much that I couldn't even hold my pen to take notes. Criticism had always made me feel very small and kind of dirty. I hoped that the Rachel's Vineyard people weren't going to guilt-trip any of us.

At our first meeting, the facilitator, Janice, reminded us that we were not allowed to tell anyone about who was there and what they had to say. You could practically hear everyone sigh a deep breath of relief. We all understood. This was the privatest of matters.

I looked around at the small group of ladies and was surprised to see that they weren't all young girls. One lady looked older than my mother! What could she have wanted there? Over time, I would learn that many women suffer severe feelings of guilt and loss after an abortion, and they come to these weekends to find emotional healing. That lady had suffered for years. She had had four more children, but she still remembered the loss of her aborted baby. I wanted badly to tell her about the cherubim, but I knew I couldn't. Deep inside, I thanked God for my short-cut. My life could have turned out a lot like that lady's life.

I learned that Melody had also had good intentions when she had her abortions. (It turned out she had had two.) Her mother had gotten pregnant with her before finishing high school and had never been able to leave the housing project.

"My mom got pregnant at sixteen because she didn't want to live under her mother's roof anymore," Melody started. "In those days, the welfare would give you your own apartment if you had a baby. She thought it was gonna be great because she'd have lots of freedom. She didn't realize that a baby isn't a toy doll that you can put down and forget about when you want to go dancing with your friends. She got through the first years okay, and when I was old enough to be left alone, she started dating again. I have two little brothers now, and I mostly take care of them myself. I think that's another reason why I won't have kids until I get on my own two feet and can live outside the projects. I watch them go out and play or go to school, and I worry that something bad might happen to them. It's not that my mom doesn't care. I think she just doesn't realize how bad it is out there for little kids. Or she doesn't know what to do about it.

"By the time I was fourteen, all the girls were talking about doing it with different boys, and they said you couldn't get pregnant the first time anyway. We felt pretty grown up and thought doing it was very cool. I don't know how *they* got away with it without getting pregnant. I got caught the first time. I knew I couldn't take care of a baby, and I didn't want to leave school or anything. Getting an abortion was a no-brainer for me. I figured I had made a mistake, but it wasn't ever going to happen again.

"After that, I was real careful not to get pregnant. The boys started calling me Condom Melody, but I didn't care. I wasn't taking any chances. Percy, the guy I was dating when I got pregnant the second time—this year—wanted kids real bad. He didn't like the idea that I wanted to raise them in a better place. To him, the projects were home, and what was good enough for him was good enough for any kid of his. I hoped that he'd see that I was right over time. I was always pointing out the bad things going on in the projects and told him how much I worried about my little brothers. I guess he was hoping I'd see things his way. Anyway, I'm pretty sure he used a bad condom.

"When I found out I was pregnant, I thought he'd panic. Instead, he wanted to get married right away. He sure didn't want me to have an abortion. He couldn't even understand why I was so mad at him. I was mad at myself, too, for trusting him. From now on, it's birth control pills for me. I set an alarm to take them at seven every morning, just to be sure. Nothing is gonna keep me from becoming a hair-dresser and making a good living before I have to think about having kids."

One of the other girls said, "When I went to see about giving up my baby for adoption, they had a class about STDs. They said you really have to be careful about them. My doctor told me the best thing is to be celibate until you find the man of your dreams."

Melody answered wryly, "I found the man of my dreams, and *he's* celibate! He's never gonna get married. What do you think of that?"

I said, "You'll find another man. Don't worry." Right away, I was sorry I had said it.

Melody gave me a dirty look.

Janice changed the subject, and the group continued sharing. We weren't required to talk about our histories or our feelings. The whole program was open and receptive. Everything they did for us was dignified and solemn—with a stress on God's love for all his people and his great ability to forgive. After hearing about the difficult decisions others had made in having their abortions, I thought I could tell my story.

"It was different for me," I started. "I did the baby a favor when I had the abortion. It was probably going to have serious birth defects because I was on a lot of drugs and so was Sam. If I gave it up for adoption, who knows what kind of life it might have had, especially if it had birth defects. And I couldn't take care of it, so abortion was the only solution. I didn't have any misgivings.

"I really liked Sam. We met in the psych ward. He was a sociopath. I thought I could help him by being his friend, and once I got to know him, I really liked him a lot. He told me not to trust him, but I couldn't believe that he could hurt me—"

"Wait! You were in a psych ward?" Melody interrupted. "Don't they keep everybody locked up? How did you all get together?"

I had to smile. "The ward is locked up, but the individual rooms aren't. We weren't quite that dangerous, I guess. We still had to be creative. I was on the women's side, and Sam was on the men's. There was a day room in the middle, and there was always someone watching us in the day room. We had single rooms, so once he got into my room, we were pretty safe. The problem was getting him in.

"We waited until after lights out. You're not supposed to hang out in your room during the daytime. He snuck into my room by crawling behind the couches and chairs in the day room. One of our friends was pretending to have a crisis, so the nurse was distracted enough that he made it. We used a different person each time, so no one would get suspicious. And we did it. Very quietly, but it was still nice. He was my first and only man. I had to do something about the blood on the sheet, so I pretended that I had started my period and apologized a lot. I got away with it."

I had everyone's attention.

"I found out I was pregnant after I got home. I had Sam's phone number, we said we'd get together after we got out. When I called him, I got his answering machine and left a message about being pregnant. Of course, he didn't call back."

There were chuckles all around.

I said, "I know. I think I've always been like that—just blurting out what I'm thinking and not thinking of the consequences of my words. Pretty dumb, huh?"

Everyone nodded.

"At first, I was happy about being pregnant. I mean, I was twenty-four. I'd had a really bad time with depression for years. It seemed like I was beginning a whole new chapter. When Sam didn't call, I started to get scared. I talked it over with my doctor. She was the one who mentioned the problem with the drugs. I knew it, but I didn't want to face it. I made plans to abort it. It was the only logical thing to do. I was doing it for the baby—not for myself—so it was easier to take. Someone told me you could abort a baby with a coat hanger. I tried to imagine how you could do that." I looked around. "Any ideas?"

No one spoke.

"Anyway, I decided not to try it. I still wanted to be able to have children someday. I went to an abortion clinic instead. I signed the papers and had it done. It was really easy."

"How did you feel afterward?" Janice asked.

"I knew there would be a feeling of loss and the depression would come back, so I kept really busy. I finally figured out what I wanted to do with my life. I sent off for college applications and took courses at the community college. I hardly thought about the baby after that. It was like a closed chapter. But now—"

"But now?" Janice said.

"Well, now I know that I was wrong all along. I was wrong to encourage Sam in the first place. It was stupid to think I could help him. That was the reason why we had sex: I was just trying to show him that he could be trusted and that he was worthy of someone's love. When I realized I was pregnant, I was foolish enough to think that having a baby would straighten out my life and end my depression. I know that having an abortion is a sin, but I couldn't have raised the baby and would have had to give it up for adoption. Who knows what kind of life it might have had? Too many things were wrong with the idea."

"How do you feel about having committed a sin?" Janice asked.

"After the abortion, God started to bug me."

"You mean your conscience?"

"Well, maybe my conscience," I said. "I was always interested in the religion of the Native Americans, and I also looked into Buddhism, but I didn't find my answer until I turned to Jesus. For me, maybe because I always went to Catholic schools, Christianity was the religion of choice. I turned to God, and he forgave me. I love the fact that God continues to forgive us—no matter what we do wrong." I wiped the tears from my eyes.

It turned out that it wasn't hard to talk about it. Maybe my story would give someone hope. I was kind of happy about the way it came out. During one of the activities, we got to name our babies. I thought about naming mine Sammy, after the father, but at the last minute, I chose Joe, after my good friend in Gainesville. It was no surprise that Melody named one of hers Ray. She named the other one after her mother, Jacklyn.

When I was alone in my room at the retreat house the night after I told my story, the Holy Spirit reminded me about my first visit from Mary. Suddenly, I knew the baby she was holding was my own. I started to cry. It was hard to keep it quiet, but I didn't want anyone in the other rooms to hear. I fell asleep crying, and Mary came to me in my dream. She unwrapped the blue blanket and showed me the little cherub, wrapped up in his little wings. He was a beautiful baby, and I was really sorry about my mistake. I held him, and it was like the time I had held Baby Jesus in Old Bethlehem. I felt a bond of love that I would never forget. I guess the romantics would call it a bittersweet memory.

When Ray picked us up on Sunday, both of us could report that we had had a good weekend. Neither of us provided details, and he chose not to ask any questions, so it was a quiet drive back to town.

"Should I drop you off at home, Melody?" he asked.

"Yeah. I guess that would be okay," she replied.

"You'll have to tell me where to go," he said.

Melody started laughing nervously.

"Yeah, I'd like to tell you where to go," she said with a grin. She gave him the directions without any more comments. In front of her building, she said, "Thanks for this, both of you. I know you care about me. I need some time to think about everything." She paused. "Don't come looking for me anymore. When I know what's going on, I'll look you up."

She gave me a light hug. There were tears in her eyes as she turned to leave.

Ray rushed up to her, took her by the shoulders, and gave her a gentle hug. He said, "God bless you, Melody. I know everything will work out, and I'm holding you to that promise to keep us posted about how things are going."

As we walked back to the apartment after parking the van at the center, Ray said, "Well, it looks like that was a successful weekend."

I answered, "Maybe. Who knows if Melody got the same out of the weekend as I did? I guess she and I are closer now, but who knows what that will mean for our relationship? Who knows if she'll return to the center? I believe she wants to keep in touch, but maybe too much has passed between us for her to feel comfortable seeing either of us."

"You don't expect her to come back to the center?"

"I don't know. We know a lot about her…things she wouldn't want anyone to know. I don't know how she'll handle that."

"It's true," Ray said. "Maybe I'll have to go somewhere else to give her some space."

Maybe he was right. "Let's see what happens between now and Easter. God will let us know what to do," I said. I didn't want to miss out on my initiation into the Catholic church when it was so close!

We didn't check on Melody. We knew she didn't want that, but I overheard conversations at the center that made me feel good about what we had done. Melody's friends had a lot to say about her.

When someone wished Melody were there to play volleyball, one of the boys said, "She ain't interested in volleyball. All she wants to do is finish high school and go to beauty school." He pranced around the gym and pretended to primp his hair.

"You should see what she can do with a head of hair!" a girl said. "I'm gonna have my hair done by her when she's in school. And after she finishes, I'm gonna be her first customer, wherever she's working. I bet she could even do something with your mop, Louis."

One day, Melody dropped in at the center after school. She approached Carol for information on how to apply to beauty school. She told her she was passing all her classes and wanted to get started as soon as possible after graduation.

Carol gave her the information and told her she could have a small room in the center to practice on hair if she wanted. Melody accepted the offer and left the center with a broad smile.

"Things are looking up," Carol said as she sat down next to me. She told me about Melody's visit. "I don't know what you guys did, but it made a big difference."

"It wasn't us, Carol," I said. "It was God."

"You're right! Praise God!" Carol gave me high five and returned to her work.

After a few days, Melody returned to the center. She was like a different person. She was friendlier and more confident. She seemed like she was a person on a mission. After greeting her friends, she went straight to Carol's office and asked about her beauty salon.

Carol explained that it would be a simple room where she could work on hair. There wouldn't be a special chair or a sink. She would have to get along with the furniture that was available. She could use the ladies' room to wash hair, as long as she didn't take up too much time there. Melody seemed satisfied.

She approached me and pulled out a chair. "Can I sit here?"

"Of course," I answered. I had been sitting alone at my table, trying to write down the words of a new song on paper. I moved my writing things aside.

"I know we're not supposed to talk about this, but I have to know something," she said. "Did you try to have an abortion with a coat hanger?"

"Absolutely not! Can you imagine how someone could manage that?"

"No. And why should anyone bother? Unless they want to hurt themselves."

"Ya. Some people get something out of hurting themselves. I did…for a long time." I rolled up my right sleeve and showed her the big scar. "I held my arm over the burner of the electric stove. I didn't touch it, but I held my arm close to it for as long as I could stand it. After a few minutes, I did it again. It helped ease the emotional pain I was in. Then, I had to go for debridement for weeks. The pain from having the dead tissue removed also helped with my emotional pain, but the relief never lasted long. I also cut myself, so I could watch the blood. That was good, too. But when it came to doing an abortion with a coat hanger, it was really too morbid. I didn't want to mess up my chances of having kids someday. I call all my scars battle scars now. I'm kind of proud of the fact that I won the battle. But I never wanted to permanently damage myself."

"So you don't hurt yourself anymore?"

"Nope. I don't need to. I'm almost always happy now, and when I get sad, it's not so bad that I can't talk myself out of it."

"Well," Melody said, "I do it."

I reminded myself to pretend ignorance. "Do what?" I asked.

"I cut myself."

"To make yourself feel better?"

"Yeah."

"Do you still need it?"

"Yeah." She paused. "How did you learn to stop?"

I died.

Since I couldn't say that, I asked the Holy Spirit to help me. I said, "I went to a two-month training program where they concentrated on getting people to stop. You have to *want* to stop, though. If you don't, you probably won't succeed. It's like an addiction, you know. Do you really want to stop?"

"Yeah. I know it's an addiction—and yeah, I really want to stop."

"I'm sure they have information here about that. Should I ask for you?"

"Don't tell Ray. I still like him a lot, and I don't want him to know."

"Okay. I'll ask Carol. Do you want to wait or come back tomorrow?" Maybe she didn't want to come every day. "Or any day?"

"I'll come back," Melody said as she got up to leave.

"Okay. I'll be here till Easter, for sure."

"Easter? That's coming up." "Yup."

"And then where will you go?"

"Home. I'm only here for a visit."

"Lucky for me—my secret will go with you."

I smiled. "Yup. Have a nice day."

"You too." Melody left quietly.

I waited until she was gone, and then I asked Carol about self-mutilation counseling. She gave me the name and number of a therapist who could help, and she promised to watch out for Melody after I left.

I made her promise not to mention Melody's situation to Ray.

"He already suspects, but she doesn't want him to be told," I explained.

"Her secret's safe with me," Carol said.

EPILOGUE

Before Easter, I had to go with my RCIA class to meet the bishop. He was satisfied with all of us and gave the okay for us to be accepted into the church at the Easter Vigil service. On Saturday, April 22, I was accepted into the Catholic church at Our Lady of Guadalupe Church.

The water was freezing as Father Eugene baptized me with three jugfuls, pausing to refill the jug each time. "I baptize you in the name of the Father (one jugful over my head), and of the Son (second jugful), and of the Holy Spirit (third jugful)."

I could hear everybody giggling and looked up, smiling. I saw Melody watching from way in the back. After changing out of my wet baptismal dress and into my Easter outfit, I was confirmed.

Father Eugene swiped a wide strip of holy oil across my forehead. (I couldn't have cared less about zits at that point.)

During Mass, I received my First Holy Communion—the Body and Blood of Jesus. Although I had already experienced God's presence in me, it was still something special. As I swallowed the wafer and drank from the cup, I felt like Jesus was becoming part of my body as well as my soul. It filled me with warm fuzzies and a strong urge to share his love.

Right after Mass, I felt compelled to hug everybody I knew. And I ran to hug Melody and say goodbye to her before she could disappear into the exiting crowd.

Later that evening—really it was the middle of the night—I said goodbye to Ray and Carol and returned home. I had really grown a lot in the Spirit, and I was anxious to learn everything else the Lord had to teach me. I wouldn't be leaving heaven for a long time, and I couldn't be any happier about that.

www.ingramcontent.com/pod-product-compliance
Lightning Source LLC
LaVergne TN
LVHW041938070526
838199LV00051BA/2834